Robert Cameron Rogers

Will o' the Wasp

A Sea Yarn of the War of '12

Robert Cameron Rogers

Will o' the Wasp
A Sea Yarn of the War of '12

ISBN/EAN: 9783337010232

Printed in Europe, USA, Canada, Australia, Japan

Cover: Foto ©Andreas Hilbeck / pixelio.de

More available books at **www.hansebooks.com**

" ' T was a well-aimed broadside, and brought
our maintop to the deck."

(*See page 211.*)

Will o' The Wasp

A Sea Yarn of the War of '12

*Edited by Henry Lawrence, U.S.N.,
and now brought before the public
for the first time*

BY

Robert Cameron Rogers

PUBLISHED, 1896, IN NEW YORK AND LONDON,
BY G. P. PUTNAM'S SONS

The Knickerbocker Press, New Rochelle, N. Y.

CONTENTS

" There is a rumor that an English frigate went into Cadiz much crippled, and with a very severe loss in men, about this time, and that she reported her injuries to have been received in an engagement with a heavy American corvette the latter disappearing so suddenly in the night that it was thought she had sunk."

COOPER'S *Naval History*
(Respecting the fate of the *Wasp*).

WILL O' THE WASP.

Wasp Willy.

A PROLOGUE.

I WAS second officer aboard the U. S. sloop-of-war *Dahcotah*, in the year 1866. We were attached to the North Atlantic squadron, and in June of the year, one afternoon in the early part of the month, lay to for a few hours off the little North Devon town of Clovelly. I had obtained permission to go ashore, spend a few days, and rejoin at Plymouth, and it was with keen pleasure that I donned "cits" and took my place in the cutter.

Our flag hung from the spanker gaff, and as it flew straight north in the wind, I never saw it look more beautiful. It may be I felt more than common pleasure in the bunting at that time, for it had just weathered one of the fiercest wars of the century, and was now flying in the breeze of a land which, despite all ties of blood, had been little better than an enemy.

It was with surprise then, that, attracted by an exclamation of the coxswain, I followed the direction of his gaze and saw a singular sight.

On the landing stage towards which our boat was headed, stood an old man, gaunt and tall, clad in rough blue serge ; upon his head a sailor's cap that might have graced the brow of some seaman of Decatur's time. His white beard fell like a frill from his pointed chin and spread almost from one ear to the other. Over his right shoulder, and this was what had stirred the coxswain's wonder, he carried a flag, faded and minus many stars in its blue field, but still the gridiron. He was surrounded by a rabble of half-grown lads, some laughing at him, some jeering. At his elbow stood a grave and stalwart middle-aged woman. The old man, whose eyes were fixed upon us as we neared the landing, paid no heed to his tormentors, but now and again the woman, making a little run, would fetch some lout of a boy a sounding cuff upon the ear, at which the yells of laughter would be tempered with rage. As I stepped from the boat, the strange old figure, paying no deference to me—I was in civilian's garb,—pushed by and hailed the coxswain.

"God be praised!" he shouted, bringing his flag to an order with a wild flourish, "you 're the first Yankee man-o'-war's-men I 've seen in twenty year. What 's the news, what 's the news, mates?—I 'm William Fry, seaman, of the United States sloop *Wasp*—on parole. What 's the news, bullies? Did n't we sink that steam pirate, hay? I can't hear ye—I 'm gettin' old."

The men, laughing, looked towards me as the one to do the talking, and the coxswain called:

"There 's the lieutenant, mate, ask him."

The old sea-dog turned at once to me and pulled at a wisp of hair that still represented his forelock.

"I ask yer pardin, sir," he said, " I did n't know you in the shore togs—I 'm William Fry, of the sloop *Wasp*, Captain Blakely, sir—on parole. Ask your pardin, sir, for letting my jaw tackle run, but I haint seen the gridiron, only this 'ere one I got, thirty year ago, till now, nor a boat crew of Yankee man-o'-war's-men in the Lord knows when. *Wasp*, sir, Cap'n Blakely, did ye know him, sir? I be'n here a prisoner of war God knows how long—on parole now, on parole."

" Hi, Wasp Willy! Wasp Willy! Yankee Bill wi' a crack in his crown!" yelled the mob of boys behind him. In a sudden rage the old man flew about and charged the group, who scattered with redoubled yells.

" There you go, you bloody young sons of rock rabbits! I 've chased yer fathers afore ye, jest that way, damn yer eyes!" He came back swearing and breathless and apologetic.

"You see, sir, my girl here, this is her; Jane Fry,—Lieutenant—what 's the name, sir?"

" Lawrence."

" Lawrence. She repels boarders mostly, for me, but they get too much for the old blood sometimes. Yes, sir, I 'm seventy-seven years old; seventy-seven I am, an' twenty-five was I when I shipped aboard the *Wasp* with Captain Blakely. Did ye say ye knew him?"

Know Blakely! Yes, I knew him, as every schoolboy who read and re-read Cooper's *Naval History*, and swore, after a whipping, to run away to sea, knew him. Blakely, of the *Wasp*—the second ship of that fighting name,—which sailed from Portsmouth in my grandfather's day, took and burned a dozen prizes, fought and whipped the *Reindeer*, fought and sunk the *Avon*, and then disappeared,—some said in the stress of a fearful fight, or the grip of a storm.

The old man did n't give me time to reply. " Ask your pardin again, sir," he said, "but might I ask some of my mates here to take a glass with me, yonder, sir, to the Blue Bell tavern—just a step?" The men looked at me inquiringly. There was no reason for denying the request. Here was I, in no hurry, off duty, and eager to see a little of the people in this quaint town. I could wait a few minutes, and chat with a couple of battered worthies who had drawn near.

"Well, go, lads," I said. "Be back in a quarter hour; I'll watch the boat—Jim, you can go too."

The men with alacrity sprang ashore, and the old sailor, forgetting me at the moment, started briskly towards the street, his daughter at one side, the flag waving above his head, and a knot of brown-faced seamen rolling in his wake. It was a quaint procession, and I laughed outright. A grizzled fisherman stood near me, and laughed too. "Who is that old lad, my man?" I asked.

"Why, zur, it's one they call Wasp Willy, or Will o' the Wasp, an' Will o' the Wisp, some do. 'E's gone wrong in his tops, zur, but a good, harmless old lad. 'E 's lived here or hereabout, at Bidevor or Combe-Martin, or here, fifty odd year."

" Is he what he says he is? No one ever came back from the *Wasp's* last cruise but the men on a prize ship." The old man rubbed his head.

" Wy, zur," he said, " 'e says so—and none can deny him—'e gets that rusty an' takes on so. Then his girl Jane 's a good true soul, and she says as how the old man has a book, a kind o' log-book, zur, as tells as how 'e was took an' how his ship went down. An' 'e 's served somewhere sure enough, zur, for he used to make pretty play in a broadsword match when he was a younger man. 'E 's handled the cutlass, zur, an' no mistake."

Further questioning brought out the fact that this curious old relic had for the last twenty years been under the impression that he was a prisoner of war, upon parole. All statements that England and America were at peace were lost upon him. He did not quite realize the meaning of the war between

the States, but he was aware, from being
gibed at various times by hangers-on at the
tavern, that there was a ship called the *Ala-
bama* sinking our merchant marine. While
we talked, a noise of cheering and laughter
came from the street. The old seaman had
come out of the tavern, was swinging flag in
one hand, cap in the other, and cheering
lustily. Then he would laugh, and shake his
fist at a group apparently within the tavern,
whose door stood open. His words were
borne to me with distinctness:

"Sunk 'er in one hour—hear that, ye
lobster catchers! Sunk 'er in one hour, an'
lost but one man—hear me, ye liars! Half
her crew was English—English, d' ye hear!
Gunners trained aboard yer ships in Portsmouth. They never *could* shoot! Sunk
the *Alabamy!* Could n't do it, hay?—In
just an hour! Come on, mates, we 'll have
one more."

I saw him turn, gather a couple of my blue-
jackets into his wide embrace, and force
them, with no great difficulty, towards the

tavern door again. To my relief they came out almost at once and hurried laughing towards the gig.

" Why, sir," said the coxswain, as he came up, " that there Billy is an old sailor, sure enough ; he 's got arms that beat anything I ever see. *Wasp* tatooed on one arm, an' *Essex* on it too. He says he served with Porter an' came home on a prize crew from the South Seas. An' the boss up to the tavern says the old lad 's a man-o'-war's-man an' no fooling. I said he 'd better join us an' go home, but he says he 's goin' to be exchanged. He 's inside now quarrelling with a half dozen swabs who he swears lied to him 'bout the *Alabamy* fight. I guess the old man 's genuine, sir—he talks man-of-war all right."

" Did you ask him how he came here ? "

" Yes, sir—said he was took in 1814 an' landed in Plymouth—heard there was a place called Bideford, and as he came from Biddeford down in Maine, he thought he 'd steer for that there port. There he got

married to some girl he says was called
Gunner Nancy, or some such name, an' had
fought aboard a British ship—oh, he 's crazy
enough, sir, some ways, I 'll bet, an' he 's
got the prettiest cutlass scar across his nut I
ever see."

When the gig had pushed off I took my
way up into the rambling town, that looks
like a little city from South Italy dropped
out of the lap of some cyclone on to the
North Devon coast. I wanted to see more
of Will o' the Wasp, and I was not disap-
pointed. Just before I reached the door of
the "Bluebell," out he came, his daughter
still following him closely. He was plainly
flushed by his liquor and the stirring news of
the last few minutes. He carried on a loud
monologue as he strode up the street, his old
cap pulled over his eyes, and the flag flaunt-
ing across his shoulder. He was still glory-
ing in the account of the *Kearsarge's* fight
and spreading curses in a broadcast manner
for all who had ever doubted its result. He
was truculent in word and bearing, so truc-

ulent, that a remnant of his persecutors, upon being charged by him and sent briskly to the lower world, left him quite alone. I saw that people of mature years looked at him with kindliness and good-humor, and several spoke pleasantly to his daughter as she toiled up the steep street about a rod behind. At last he reached his own house, one of a score like it in Clovelly—low door, and stone threshold well-worn, narrow windows, and a platform outside the door from which one might view the sea. He went inside with a bang to of the door. In a moment an upper window opened, the flag came through, and the sash closed upon the staff, holding it in place. I was at the woman's side as she reached the house. She recognized me, and curtsied, looking, as I thought, a little shamefaced.

"Tell me," I said, "how much of what your father says is true, and what is fancy?"

"About his being in the wars, sir?"

"Yes—the war between England and America in 1812."

"Why, sir, I think that 's mostly true, sir
—the rector, sir, comes sometimes and talks
wi' him, an' he says as how it sounds true,
an' my mother—she died when I was but a
child—used to say 't was all as father made
out.   Some days, sir, he 's strange, an' to-
day 't was the ship an' the flag, an' all, mazed
him a bit, an' his drink, sir—it 's that I 'm
fearful of, for it does always maze him cruel.
You see, sir, he 's been hit hard on the head
when a young man, an' when he 's excited he
goes very queer at times."

"Well, how about that diary—that log-
book of his cruise in the *Wasp?* " I asked.

"He 's got it sir, an' keeps it under lock
an' key in his chest.   He swears it 'll be
worth money some day for history; but
Lord, sir, 't will but be fit for to kindle a
fire, I fear."

"Still," I said, "there may be something
interesting and valuable in it, anyhow to an
American sailor.   Here is my name, and this
will be my address the next two weeks.   If
your father cares to part with that journal you

can drop me a line, for I 'll be this way again in a fortnight, and if it 's curious, as I guess it will be, I 'll make you an offer."

.   .   .   .   .   .

Ten days later, to my address in Exeter, came a letter and a parcel. The letter ran:

"LIEUTENANT LAWRENCE: SIR,—My father's health was very bad after you left. 'T was the drink and excitement, I fear. A week later he was took serious and died. He left me all but his flag—that he had wrapped round him in his coffin—and his book. He told me and made me promise solemn to give this, his log, he called it, to you, for I told him what you 'd asked me, and he was set upon its being made into history. I found much in it that was private-like about himself and mother, and asked him to let me keep that back, but he says, ' 't is all a part of the cruise of the *Wasp*, and all goes or none,' and he made me swear solemn to send it to you. If you think it worth anything you may give me what you think is right, and when you may be done with it, please send it to me again. I live in the old house to Clovelly.   " Yours respectfully,

                              " JANE FRY."

After reading the journal, I sent what turned out to be a satisfactory remuneration. I made up my mind to edit it upon my own responsibility, as a chapter in the history of the last war with England never opened before, and as a romance as well. The diary, which is in many places a sort of auto-biography, was apparently written some years after the events described took place, and is based upon the data of a log kept by the old seaman during his service upon the *Wasp*. It has the ring of truth about it, though for its authenticity none can vouch. It gives one a version of the end of the gallant Blakely and his sloop-of-war that I for one am glad to adopt. I have tried as closely as may be to retain the seaman's idiom and syntax, while turning the entire story into a coherent narrative. For what it may be worth then, as history, or, as they say in the Navy, a good yarn, I submit it to the public.

HENRY LAWRENCE.

U. S. N.

CHAPTER I.

HOW I SIGNED WITH CAPTAIN BLAKELY.

OF all lucky cruises, so far as I and my mates thought, Captain Porter's in the South Seas was luckiest—till he struck the rock he split on in Valparaiso Bay.

It was nothing but prize, prize, prize; whalers and merchantmen; with just a smell of powder, now and again, to keep the gunners in good temper. The Captain and the folks in the ward-room worried sometimes, I 've heard, about meeting nothing of our size to lay alongside; but as for me, I was content as things ran.

They got all the fight they wanted, later on, and took it like the game cocks they were.

You can't make me see much to brag on in that fight off Valparaiso. Two to one and long range! They never dared come aboard,

and a neutral harbor too! But that 's John
—that 's his way. If there 's something to
be gained, why, it 's " Damn neutrality in a
nation I can whip ! "

But it was my fortune to be put aboard
the *Hector*, merchantman, in a prize crew and
sent home long before the fight, and home I
got in due time, and found myself the spring
of 1814 in Portsmouth town, pockets full of
money and a good opinion of myself as well,
and both these facts, as I shall tell, brought
me to ship aboard the *Wasp*. I was minded
to lay by for a few months. I had plenty
money yet to make a merry summer of it,
and had sent home a tidy sum, as well, to
Biddeford, for I 'm a down Easter. I had n't
the notion of going to sea again till I had to,
and I knew the *Wasp*, that they 'd been trying to get me to ship aboard, was going out
for fighting. I knew all about Blakely, her
captain, and what kind of a man he was.

Now, I don't call myself a coward, and the
one man that ever did I whipped till he took
it back; but life 's a good thing, and shore,

if you have some money about you, is pleasant after a long cruise, and though I was willing to fight, I was n't the sort who 'd rather do it than eat. Thinks I : " While I can find a white dollar by looking in my pockets, I won't go a-seeking it to sea. When the money goes I 'll go too, and the war 's good to last a good year more, I guess." So I would n't ship.

There were a parcel of 'em after me. I was a good-looking young man, I reckon. Six foot I stood in my stockings, and though not very broad, I was deep and wiry. I was but twenty-five, and my habits, bar a frolic now and then, were good.

Well, there was a lad I knew, a town lad, in a dry-goods store in Portsmouth, that I 'd had a little trouble with. He and I were courting the same girl, a nice girl she was, and a daughter of old Aaron Truby of River Street. Well, she liked me best, though the other—Jim Downs was his name—sung in the choir ; and so Jim ships aboard the *Wasp* and tries to get me to come along.

2

"Bill," says he, one day, down on the wharf,
"I'm going to sea in the trimmest, sweetest
craft you ever clapped your lights on "—he
was quick to pick up the lingo he didn't
half understand,—" and her captain's the
king-pin of the lot," says he. " Why don't
you ship with us? You're an old man-o'-
war's-man by your own account."

"Steady," says I, " by my mates' account,
as well."

" Oh, no offence," he says, laughing. " Only
I thought maybe you'd be game for another
crack at John."

I told him how things were with me ; how
I was minded to lay off the summer; that I
had a couple of hundred dollars by me yet,
and that the war would last. He looked at
me out of the tail of his eye, as I quit talking,
and says:

" Two hundred dollars won't keep a wife,
Billy. Come along, man, and make a few
hundred more ; that 'll be hard sense," says
he.

Now this wasn't his business, and I told

him so, and told him so straight. He riled
me and always had, and I sent him along.
Off he goes looking sour, but he knew too
much to try to come aboard me. Next day I
met the boatswain of the *Wasp* with three or
four lads at his heels, one of them old Josh
Sewall, who 'd fought aboard the *Bon Homme
Richard* in '79, and who knew me well. I
saw boatswain tip Josh the wink, and the old
man comes up to me very friendly.

" Bill," says he, " we 're looking for a man
of your size," says he, " and a good, all round
seaman like you ; now, my bully," says he,
" you 're too good a man to rot in drydock,
and too young. Here 's Cap'n Blakely and
the trimmest sloop o' war that swims, from
here to Good Hope and home by way of
the Horn," says he. " Lots of prize money,
stiff fighting, maybe, for I won't lie to you,
and I know Captain Blakely ; and a well put
up man, like you, a tried seaman, as well,
may look for a lift, if others knocks under."

Well, he kept at me for maybe a quarter
hour ; they seemed bound to get me, for

when I'd shook off Josh, two other seamen
of Blakely's hove me to, and paid away the
same coil of talk.   But I was set in my own
notion, and the more they talked the closer
I stuck to it.   I see now that it began to
make me feel like a pretty big man to have
them chase me up this way, and by night
of this day I felt a little bit more than plain
William Fry. We'd have a little something
now and again to grease the tackle with, and
by night I was running free and all sail set.
Now there was a little tavern in River Street
where sailors used to go to drop a few dollars over dice, maybe, or stand a few rounds
of ale or Medford, and there that night was
I, and with me every man who'd talked
Wasp with me that day, and drink was
plenty and jaw-tackle loose. Josh Sewall had
served aboard the *Constitution*, and sang a
song going the round those days that went—

> " The *Guerrière* a frigate bold
> As e'er on foaming ocean rolled,"

and so on, telling how she could lick the

Frenchmen two to one, but how *we* whipped *her*.

Josh seemed very drunk, and kept at me all the time with : " Here 's to Cap'n Hull— here 's one to Lawrence—now Bill, I give you your old Captain, Porter," and so it went. There was nothing to do but drink. I saw I was paying right and left, but that I did n't care about. I was rich enough to stay ashore, and they were going to sea again for the rhino. By-and-by I forgot what was going on, till suddenly I was aware the bar was quiet and some one shaking me. " Sit up, Billy," says a voice, and I found I was in a chair by a table where I 'd been when I lost myself. The sailors, all but Josh, were gone, but there in the middle of the room, looking at me very black, was Aaron Truby ! How he came there I did n't at the minute know, but there he was.

" William," says he, very solemn—" I know you come to see my daughter, and till now I 've been willing it should be so ; but to-night, right here, among your mates---I may

say your betters—you boasted you would
marry her. Thank God I've seen you for
what you are. Don't come to my house
again," says he. "If it had n't been for Jim
Downs I'd never have rightly known you."

"Did that cowardly sculpin bring you
here?" I says, trying to stand up, and lurching on to the bar. "If he did, this town's too
small for the two of us, by——"

"Silence!" says he, very stern—he was a
deacon in the church, and if I had n't been
tipsy I'd never have thought to curse before
him. "Keep your oaths to yourself," says
he. "There'll be room enough in the town
for you if it's Jim you think crowds you—
he's going to fight for his country like a man
while you stay here and soak. But never
cross my door-sill again. That's all."

Out he went, and the door slammed to. I
looked at old Josh, and I thought he seemed
pretty sober for a lad who'd stowed so much
under the hatches, and he looked as if he was
a bit sorry for my raking from Aaron. Then
I felt in my pockets. Loose change there

was, copper and silver, but my gold—nigh two hundred dollars—was gone. I did n't say a word for a minute, but my face must have spoke loud enough. Then says I, very deliberate :

"Well, when I sailed along with Captain Porter in the *Essex*, there 's many a night my mates and I have set the grog going pretty free, and each man of us with a fist full of yellow boys; but the only hands that went into our pockets were our own. I 've drunk with a good many seamen," says I, getting to my feet—I was getting nigh to sober now, —"but I never lost a farthing before."

"What do you mean?" says Josh, pretty hot.

"Mean?" says I. "I mean that some swab has taken about two hundred dollars in gold coin out of my breeches while I sat here thinking I was safe among American seamen, by the Lord," says I, "that 's what I mean." He got up and took a tack or two about the room ; then he came and sat down next to me again.

"I 'm sick of this job," says he, "and I 'll
tell you how it was, Bill. You see, we
wanted you bad aboard the sloop, and I said
I'd get you, seeing there 's no press-gang,
somehow or t' other. So I says to the lads
along with me, ' We 'll get him drinking, and
get away with that chink that 's making him
hug shore, and when he finds he 's strapped,
he 'll ship. Once out to sea, we 'll hand the
money back '—sit down !"

I 'd got to my feet very savage.

" Sit down and hold your tongue till I 'm
through. Why, you 're a good man, mate,"
says he, " but you 're too unsteady on those
pins to tackle me now; sit down, I tell ye.
There, that 's right and sensible. So we got
you tight, and I took your money. Here it
is, every shilling of it—take it. And while
you snored in your chair, along comes
Downs, gives a look at you, and goes out
pretty quick. Back he steers with the old
party that just raked you. I did n't know
till then you were sparking a lass, Bill," he
says, putting his hand on my shoulder, " and

now I know it, I 'm sick of the job. Give us
your hand," says he, "and say you don't
bear a grudge."

I suppose I was turned silly by the drink,
for to find my money as sudden as I missed
it, and a staunch seaman alongside pitying
me for the mess I was in, and the blast old
Aaron gave me, together with the chance I
stood to lose my girl, made me whimper like
a baby.

" No grudge at all, Josh," says I ; "and in
a way 't was a joke I earned. But joke or no
joke, there 's no laugh in it with old Aaron
and Lindy. He 's seen me drunk, and now
he 'll believe no less than that I 'm a sot.
'T is the end of the game for me, Josh," I
says, with my knuckle in my eye like a lad
that 's been switched at school. "You don't
know the old pirate ; and Lindy, she 's nigh
as strict."

Old Josh cursed a bit to himself like, and
stood up and down the room. By-and-by he
says : " If Jim Downs comes back from this
cruise with a pocket full, and finds you here

about run out of money, and on the black
list too, he 'll weather you sure enough, Bill,"
says he.

I 'd thought of that too.

" So, lad," goes on the old man, " why not
ship as well ? "   And then after a minute, as
I sat thinking : " There 's another girl," says
he, " that you and me don't talk much of,
maybe, but we love her all the same.   Her
head 's on this coin here, and her name 's
Columbia," says he, very solemn.   " Why,
boy, there 's more than money to be got
aboard the *Wasp*.   We 're no greedy pri-
vateersmen, Bill, and when you 've been a
few days along with Captain Blakely you 'll
begin to think a man owes his country just a
little.   Now Blakely 's not born this side;
but he 's been adopted by us, and means to
show us the family can be proud of him.
Here are you and I, Bill, born here, and
raised—leastways you, for I 'm an old man
that remembers Colony days—raised free.
Why ?   Because some men thought more of
liberty and the land that bred 'em than of

their skins or property. Then Bill," he says,
" that girl of Truby's will think more of you,
and old Aaron likely will forgive you when
you come back, if you do."

" There it is, mate—*if* I do."

" Why, if you don't, Billy," says he, slap-
ping me on my shoulder, " you 'll go down
with the bravest captain that breathes, or
get a burial as fine as if you wore a sword.
You 'll have the same monument Commodore Decatur would get, and the whole wide
sea for a churchyard. Come, Bill. I 've
treated you fair, and I 'm telling you truth.
It 's the man's course I 'm setting for you,
and you know it."

Yes, I knew it. Old Josh did n't use to
talk very much, and the blast he gave me
almost winded him. Part what he said of
Jim's chances against mine with Lindy, part
the thing he spoke of—my owing the country
a duty,—and part because I was maybe a little homesick for a taste of the salt water
again, did the business for me. He saw me
weakening, and says he with a wink :

"What 's more, Downs wont be ashore
again," says he, "for we sail the day after
to-morrow, and you 'll like a crack at him for
the trick the lubber has done you."

"That settles it," says I. "I 'll ship for
the rest of the war, if it 's only to even up in
the fo'k'sle with the hound. Come along—
I 'll go aboard with you to-night. But, mate,"
says I, "I 've no kit ready."

"Don't you worry, my lad," says Josh.
"We 've got one that will suit you to a but-
ton. Why, Lord love you, Billy," says he—
and the old sea lawyer laughed suddenly till
he nigh choked,—"we meant to have you,
and I *knew* I 'd get you, so all 's ready for
you aboard. Foul did n't win, but fair does
the trick, eh, mate?"

Well, I laughed too. After all, the old lad
had been square and true. "I wont back-
water," says I.

"Well, you 'd better," says he, joking, "for
it 's a steadier horse in the end to back than
rum." And we both went out of the tavern
and along down to the wharf. A boat lay

there, and three men—one of 'em Downs—
asleep in her. "Wake up, lads!" calls Josh;
and they sat up rubbing their eyes.

"Got him, hay," says one, with a laugh.
"He came of his own free will," says Josh,
dryly, as we climbed down and aboard.

"Hobson's choice, maybe," says Jim to me,
as I took an oar. I gave him a look. "I came
because I wanted to see you about some
business, matey," says I, softly. "Something you and me will settle in the fo'k'sle,"
says I. He looked a little down at this,
but was going to give me a shot back, when
Josh, who was coxswain, sings out, "Toss,
all! No more jawing, you sneaking little
counter-jumper. Bill, shut your mouth.
Give way!"

When we were a few hundred feet from
the ship Josh says softly to me: "Look at
her," says he; "there's the best ship under
frigate class that sails the seas." I had
looked at her often before, and I turned
and looked as he spoke. She was a beauty,
—there could n't be two words about that.

She was a sloop-of-war, what they call, too,
a corvette. Three masts she had, and pretty
spars they were. She was deep in the waist
like ships of her class, and was pierced for
eleven guns to the broadside. A big brig of
war might have been her match, but 't would
have had to *be* a big one. As she lay in the
moonlight she looked nigh the size of my
old ship the *Essex* frigate, but the darkness
made her look larger than she was, for she
was not in the frigate class nor near it. As
we came alongside several seamen with a lantern among 'em peered over at us. Another
man joined them. I saw he was in officer's
uniform, and as we got aboard and Josh
saluted and called him Captain, I knew 't was
Captain Blakely himself.

"So you got him," I heard him say, as the
old man stepped aft a rod or two to report.
"Aye, aye, sir," says Josh, "but he did n't
need much urging. Says he 's wanting a job
and glad to sign." This was a lie, but I
guess the old lad wanted to make it easier
all round for me. The Captain came up to

me as I stood waiting for orders, and looked
me up and down. "You 're the man I
wanted," says he, after a minute. " What 's
your age ? "

" Twenty-five, sir."

" Good. We 've work ahead for young
men" (he was only thirty-four himself).
" Born in Portsmouth ? "

" Biddeford, sir."

" It 's just as good," says he ; " my men
are all Yankees, and you 'll be in good company." He turned on his heel and went
aft. Josh followed him. I heard them laugh
and I guess 't was at my cost, but now I 'd
made my mind up to ship I did n't care, and
truth to tell it pleased me to find they 'd
been at such pains to get me. I was given
a hammock and turned in at once.

Next day I kept aboard ship. I sent a
letter to my folks in Biddeford, telling them
I 'd gone again to sea. I knew 't would n't
trouble them. I 'd always been a rover—
not a black sheep, mind you, but one who 'd
jump a fence whether the bell-wether showed

the way or not. I sent them part of my
money, and some I gave to an old shipmate,
Caleb Whaley, who was going ashore, to
buy a little gold charm I told him of.   He was
to take it, with a few lines, to Lindy Truby.
Maybe she could n't read the letter, my fist
was never proper squared for writing, but she
would know what the brooch meant.   When
Caleb came aboard that night and told me
how she looked when she got it and the news
of me shipping aboard the *Wasp*, I was glad
I 'd stayed on the sloop. She did n't take
on as I thought she might, and, to tell the
truth, hoped she would. She said she guessed
it was a good thing for me.   And then, by
Caleb's account, she was very sociable with
him.   He could n't say enough about her,
which is to say he said too blasted much,
and I was glad I 'd stayed aboard. Says I
to me :

"Well, there 's always a gain somewhere.
Here 's Captain Blakely has a likely seaman
through this mess you 've made, Bill, and a
cabin-boy too, for Downs is in the same

snarl. Cabin-boy!" says I, chuckling to myself, for I thought the notion smart; " that 's what Jim 's good for, and naught besides." I met him a few minutes later on the deck, rigged out very fine in his sea togs, proud as a boy in his first boots. He did n't look happy as I came up to him, but he leaned up against the bulwarks and tried to face me out.

" Jim," says I, " I was going to settle a little score with you to-day that might have spoiled your good looks," says I, " but I 've thought better of it. You tried to ruin my chance with Lindy! Well, I never had any, I guess—anyhow, if I had, I 'm glad it 's gone. If I lived to grow gray in Portsmouth town, she might die an old maid now before I 'd help her out. Thank you, Jim," says I, " you 've done me a good turn where you meant a foul. But hark ye, mate, don't run across my bows again," I says, " for I might forget you are five foot five and I six foot," and I turned and left him very quiet. He looked pretty thoughtful all that day. I

3

guess he began to suspicion that Lindy liked shop-clerks and choir-singing better than sailors, and kind of longed to be ashore and tuning up in the old meeting-house. But 't was too late now, and early morning of May 1st heard the boatswain's whistle piping lively and saw us stand out to sea.

A crowd watched us go. There were fathers and mothers and sweethearts, all to see us sail. I did n't see Lindy, and I told myself I did n't care. Yet I felt a little as if I 'd like to have had some claim to a foot of the white bunting that kept going up to women's faces or flapping from their hands. 'T was a sad sight too, but 't is Jack's life, and after all, would he change it? Not while the sight 's good, and the muscles stringy and hard, and foothold steady, and the sea winds blow.

CHAPTER II.

WE got safe away to sea, and that might ha' been a trick none too easy. There was a big squadron cruising along the coast, shutting up in port some of our best ships. But Captain Blakely had made up his mind to get to sea and to sea we got. I daresay a 74-gun ship might have blocked him, though he 'd ha' sailed all around her in a light breeze, but I don't think he 'd have stopped for any single frigate. He was out to fight. To cut up British shipping all he could of course, but to fight first, last, and all the time.

There was something about the course he laid and the cruising ground he made straight for, that told us men we had work cut out.

35

Just as a bull terrier goes straight to a leg or
the throat, so the *Wasp* ran straight for the
Chops of the Channel. No cruising in Southern Seas. No coasting, nor waiting in our own
waters for the Englishmen to come and find
us. As fast as sails and a true course could
make it we went to the very navy-yard of
Great Britain, to the narrow seas, where the
merchantmen were thick and men-o'-war ran
plenty.

I did n't think he 'd lay the course he did,
but Josh, who was very chummy with me,
says:

"Bill," says he, "don't you mistake me.
He carries a chip on his shoulder, and he 's
going to give John a dare in John's own
water. Cruise awhile in the South Seas do
you say, man? Why, there 's more prizes,
anyway better, where we 're going. Not
dirty, stinking whalers, lad, but good, fat
Indiamen, and then, as I 've said before,
there 's no danger of our guns a-rusting.
Who 's that singing below?"

I knew the voice,—'t was Jim Downs.

The poor beggar had been sick as a land-cat
for the first two or three days' run. If he 'd
had a heart in him, or a soul he 'd ha'
parted with it those few days. Now he was
better, and stirring round a bit. He wa'n't
fit for a seaman, but they used him as a kind
of assistant purser's clerk, for he was handy
with his pen. 'T was he singing, very mourn-
ful and yet sweet too, for he had a good
voice, do him that justice. He sat upon a
chest not far from the fo'k'sle hatch. It was
something about the "sweet month of May"
he was singing, and one line ran,

" Where the cows sweetly lowing in a dewy morning." [1]

There was plenty more of it, all praising
landsman's life. He sang high up and very
sweet, and there were three or four lads,
marines, country boys I reckon, sitting round
him pretty solemn. They were young and
new to the trade, and had sweethearts to
miss 'em, maybe. *I* would n't have both-

[1] I find this song printed in the log of a privateer of the
War of Independence.   H. L.

ered him, but it riled Josh to see him sitting
there singing, and now and again piping his
eye.

"Belay there!" he shouted down the hatch.
"Stow that song, you, Downs" (he was always hard on Jim since the trick on me).
"What a hell of a song to sing aboard a
man-o'-war! You won't hear the cows
'sweetly lowing' again, lad — not soon.
You're going to see a bull, my boy, and if
you like his voice, 't is more than I guess
for," says Josh, who never lost a chance at a
joke. "Now, then, here's a song for you
boys, and I'll sing it myself. It's a song
for lads with red blood in their veins"; and
Josh, in a voice that sounded like the hoist-
ing of the mainsail, sang a song I afterwards
learned myself. It had a good swing to it,
and the words pleased us all. The marines
were cheered up by it, and even Jim Downs
sat by to listen. There was a crowd about
the old man before he finished with it. The
words were gloomy enough, but they had
the smell of salt water and tarry ropes about

'em and a breeze with 'em that made it easy
for a seafaring man to understand; then
there was a kind of daredevilry about the
song that caught the youngsters:

> " But as Providence would have it it was not quite so bad,
> But first we lost our mizzen-mast and then went off our
>   flag,
> And next we lost our main-mast, one of our guns also,
> With five men drowned then, in the Bay of Biscay O ! "

The men, such as knew it, would come in
strong on the last line, and the " five men
drowned then " pleased the green ones.
They began to think because they were
aboard ship, harking to songs about drown-
ing and the dangers of the sea, that they
were sharing some themselves. Well, God
knows they got their full ration, and it came
quick and rather sudden.

Josh Sewall was a good deal of a man
aboard the *Wasp*—he was only an ordinary
seaman, but he was an old, tried hand, a
great favorite with the quarter-deck, and his
experience, his service in three wars—the
Independence, the one against Tripoli, and

this—made him to be looked up to in the fo'k'sle. All this did n't set him up too high and keep him from being good shipmate to the youngest lad aboard. He 'd seen the *Constitution* pound the *Guerrière* into matchwood, and whip the *Java* too, but he was no hand to brag. Some of the raw hands would talk by the fathom of Perry and Decatur and Bainbridge and Hull, and what they 'd done, and I 'd say a word or two myself for Captain Porter, but Josh never took a hand in the game. The talk of our making the sea too hot for John Bull with our little navy, of how a Yankee sloop could stand off a 32, yes, or a 44 frigate, made the old man laugh.

"Wind," says he, "wind. "If you lads 'll sit just astern the mainsail you 'll fill the old sheet out and give us a knot or two to the better," says he. He knew, at sea, that what talked was gunning and good seamanship and, above all, a well disciplined crew.

"Speak of Hull and Bainbridge and the others," says he, suddenly, one day, when a

lot of us off duty were paying out talk, "all
you please, but there's never a lad of you
to say a word for Captain Lawrence, as
brave a man as ever walked the quarter-
deck."

No one had said anything of him, and
that was true. The country was still sore
over the *Shannon* taking the *Chesapeake* in
single action off Boston Harbor.

"As good a man was he," says Josh again,
"as Bainbridge or Decatur, but what ruined
him? A bad crew—a lot of raw lubbers and
foreign swabs." (Josh was veering for a ser-
mon to the new men, I saw that.) "A green
hand may be brave, but he's not worth his
grog if he don't know his trade. Hark to
that, you boys there—you, Jim Downs, I
mean you too."

"I aint a seaman," says Jim, very cool;
"I'm assistant purser's clerk."

"Lord bless you," says old Josh, rolling
his quid in his mouth, "I nor any man
aboard this ship 'll accuse *you* of being a
seaman, but if you think," and here he be-

gan to warm up, "you 'll be let off your
trick at fighting, if any one comes aboard of
us, you 've missed your guess, my bully,"
says he. "One thing about our navy, that 's
not out of its baby clothes yet, is that every
man fights if he has to. Why, the only man
on the quarter-deck when Captain Broke
came aboard the *Chesapeake* was who? Who
do you think, you purser's clerk? Why,
the chaplain, by thunder!—the parson, full
of fight, and lets go his pistol at the Britisher, and gets his arm sliced half off for it!
No, don't you fret yourself, mate—you 'll
learn to finger a cutlass as well as a pen
aboard this ship; and you other boys, remember what I say, a green hand who wont
learn is only fit for ballast, and not for that
half the time."

Josh got up and walked away. He 'd said
all he had to, given us each a shot, and he
had n't time for yarn-spinning that did n't
carry a moral along. I liked what he said
of every man doing his trick when the time
came, but as for brag, it 's my notion that a

little aint so bad.   Of course " Holdfast 's "
the better dog, but let the men crack 'em-
selves up now and again.   What has gone to
make the British the sea-dogs all know them
for?   Bull-dog grit?   Pluck, seamanship?
Yes, of course, and one thing else—the
steady belief they have that they never get
licked.   It 's always heavier metal or bloody
bad luck does the trick, or maybe it 's because the other ship is " manned half by
English sailors," or some such yarn.   Yarn
they don't think it, not for a minute, 't is
gospel to them.   The thing that 's played
the devil in their service, when fighting us,
is that their officers swallow the same windy
duff they feed the men.   Officers should
know better.   They 've no right to blink
facts to salve their pride.   Let the Jack Tars
believe they can't be whipped and never
have been, fairly; it 'll help 'em, it wont
hurt 'em anyhow, and it pleases the young
ones.   But let the officers find out and profit
by what 's wrong when they strike a foul
streak of fortune—they 'll do better next

time. As for the crew, why, let Brag bark a
little, now and again, 't will heart up old
Holdfast.

Now Josh, when I come to think, had no
right to preach. I've heard the story told
that the day Hull took the *Guerrière*, Josh
rowed bow in the first boat went off to the
prize. There were three or four American
merchant captains, prisoners aboard the Englishman. They'd come on deck when the
fight was over and one sees Josh whom he'd
known in old times.

"Well, Josh," he calls out, "what have
you folks been doing with us?" "Doing
with you!" says the old man, "been playing
with you—but if it had n't ha' been the Sab-
bath we'd ha' shown you what fighting *was*,"
says he.

Now according to my lights that's pretty
tall brag, yet it never kept old Josh from being as brave a man as ever I saw buckle on
a cutlass, bar one or two, and one is the man
I must speak of now, Captain Johnston
Blakely.

He was not a large man, but he had a figure that, in a way of speaking, was cleared for action all the time. Every muscle was taut, every pound of flesh had its use, and he carried nothing in the way of cargo. He was the soul of his ship—not of his ship's crew—I don't mean that here, though he was; but if ever a wooden ship had a soul, and I 've seen 'em look like living things, then the soul of the trimmest, staunchest, gamest sloop-o'-war that ever swam the pond, was Johnston Blakely. A polite man to every one was he. If you had done your duty, he was as civil to you, be you common seaman, as though you lived in the ward room. He was one of the breed of fighters who 'd got their schooling in Tripoli with Decatur and Somers and Bainbridge and Hull. He was born in North Ireland, but was brought a baby to the States, and now hailed from North Carolina.

He had a crew of young men like himself. The average age of the entire ship's company could n't have been more than twenty-three

years—green and raw a great part of them,
but of good stuff that seasoned soon. I 'll
never forget the first week at sea. Of all
remarkable sights on this cruise,—and there
were more than one,—what struck me as the
strangest was to see scores of the crew sick
as landsmen, leaning over the bulwarks or
lying pale and quiet on the fo'k'sle and in
their hammocks.[1] I don't blame 'em, not I.
Sick as a cat I was the first time I put to sea
in the old coaster *Hannah Fairbanks*, running
'twixt Biddeford and Boston town. All
these youngsters were trained to handle
ropes and lay aloft as brisk as ever an old
sea-dog, but they were harbor-trained.
When we got out to sea the roll and pitch
caught them hard between decks, and, as I
said, we had a floating hospital for about a
week.

But when that was past the good blood in
the boys showed forward. How they ate!

---

[1] I find corroboration of this statement in volume vii.
of Niles's *Register*, in one of the items about the *Wasp*.
                                        H. L.

'T was worth a shake-up, to gain the twist they had. And soon 't was pretty to see them get aloft and out upon the yards, lively as if they 'd followed the sea from the cradle! 'T is in the Yankee to be a good seaman. The long, long sail in the top-heavy tubs of one hundred and fifty years ago put it into the blood of their forefathers—the salt air and the sea breeze got into the blood and stayed there. So what with the knack in the blood, stout hearts, good discipline, and top-rate officers from captain to boatswain's mate, the *Wasp's* crew, by the time we were within a few days' run of the Channel, was as good a lot of seamen as I 'd ask to see. Of course many of them had seen no fighting as yet, but that 's not half the importance some reckon it.

June 2d we sighted a sail, for which we at once made chase. 'T was pretty to see the excitement among the new lads, and good for the heart to know they were looking for fight more than prize-money. Even I got a spice of the feeling that stirred them. I 'll say honest, for lying was a hitch I never learned, that a prize or two or three before long bowls, with grape and cutlass to wind up with, was more to my taste. But 't was pleasant to see those boys get aloft and shake out the canvas, and stand about the deck and pump the old hands. 'T was:

"What d' ye make her out, Josh?" and, "Is she a privateer or a brig-o'-war?" and, "Will we overhaul her, do you think?" and, "Blast her for a coward! see her run!" and all that. It pleased Josh and the other older seamen to see their spirit, and they had more than all the questions they could answer put to 'em. I came in for a share, for tho' I 'd seen but little fighting, I counted for something as a man who 'd helped take many a prize along with the *Essex* and Captain Porter. Jim Downs got a pinch of the spirit astir himself.

"Dassent wait for us, Josh," says he, edging up to the old man who 'd rarely a decent word for him. "Is she a man-o'-war, d' ye think?"

"Well," says the old lad, without looking at him, " I guess she's a ship o' the line, the *Poictiers*, maybe, or a whole fleet of warships, including gunboats and bomb-ketches," says he. "Why, you poor ignorant tune-singing deputy-purser's clerk," says he, looking round sudden, and letting go a sluice from his quid over the rail, "John does n't keep men-o'-war for races of this kind," says he; "they fight with their guns, not with their heels. Why, if that sail yonder carried the king's commission, she'd be running down here to flap it in our eyes instead of crowding all sail to get away like the poor scared merchant brig she is."

"So she is," says one of the new hands. "You never saw lines like that in a man-o'-war," says another; and Josh laughs and turns to go aft. The Captain and Lieutenant Tillinghast, a fine seamanly officer, stood talking together about midship, and eying the chase through their glasses. They beckoned Josh, and he up to them and salutes. I guess they were questioning him about the

4

excitement forward, and that the old man had his joke about the 74-gun ship over again, for they both laughed hearty. Then the Captain took a few steps towards a crowd of us standing and lying just abaft the fo'k'sle hatch. He did n't come very close, for he did n't want us jumping up and saluting, and he had n't anything to say either. But he felt good, for he was smiling, I saw that. He had a smile that drew a smile. Let him look that way at any old sour face in the crew, and 't was ten to one the smile came back at him. There was something not like other men about Captain Blakely. I always had a kind of feeling about him that—how shall I say it? Well, most men I can see in my mind growing old and leathery-faced and wrinkled, but he did n't seem to me to be a man for whom the Lord had an old age assigned, but one who had his work cut out, and that done with, good-by. But this is, likely, all my fancy.

We overhauled the brig, for brig she was,

and sent a boat's crew aboard her. Tim
Stevens was coxswain, and I rowed stroke—
a fine seaman was Tim, and my good friend.
When we came alongside, there stood the
merchant captain by the taffrail. Very sour
he looked, and small wonder, for in an hour
or two he knew the *Neptune*, which was the
name of the brig, would be sunk or burnt.
But as we climbed aboard, we had no eyes
for the captain. 'T was a girl that stood
near him we looked at.

If the captain's face was sour, what shall
I say of hers? But steady all—'t was not
sour—that it could never be, but it was
angry, and bitter angry at that. There 's a
few, a very few women have faces that look
well in a rage. She was one. " If she 's so
pretty, mad," says Tim to me," " what 'll she
be, smiling, Bill?" And I guess the point
was a good one.

While our lads busied themselves about
the prize I stood at the wheel and the Lieutenant near me ; he knew a pretty face himself, and I got a good look at the lass. She

might have been eighteen, about, and quite
tall and well put up and trim. She had eyes
of light brown that turned darker when she
looked at you. Her cheeks were red, and
brown too from the sea-wind and the sun,
and her hair that reddish brown with a yet
redder streak in it, that takes the sun free,
and has a shine of polished copper about it.

She saw me looking at her and turned
about and stood with her back towards me.
By and by she turned a bit just to see if I
was looking her way still, and when she
found 't was so, she looked prettier than ever.
Her jaw was square, and her nose what might
be called turned up, just a thought, and she
had a way of showing her teeth, white between the red of her lips, that made me think
of a terrier. I held my hand to her as she
climbed down to the cutter, but she never
saw it, or acted so. Josh Sewall helped her
down and she crouched in the stern of the
boat by the side of the brig's captain. All
this time she had n't said a word.

Now the Lieutenant saw, like the rest of

us, what a pretty bit of a craft she was, and several times he spoke to her—some little thing or other—but not a word would she give him. By and by, as the sea was coming now and again over the gunwale, he leaned over to pull a bit of tarpaulin across her knees. She jumped away from him so brisk she nigh upset the boat. The Lieutenant drew back looking kind of offended, and no wonder, and the brig captain, who did n't know what we Yankees were going to do with him, and did n't want to get our tempers going, says to her very short:

"Don't be a fool, Nancy, don't be a fool, I tell ye." Well, 't was as good as a play. She turned on him and spoke for the first time in my hearing:

"Don't *you* dare speak to me that way, you coward," she says, "don't you dare. Speak to men so, if you want to, but not to me. But you don't dare to talk so to men, not even Yankees. I 'd have sunk the boat-load of 'em this day if you 'd let me touch off the carronade."

"For God's sake hold your tongue, you
shrew," calls the brig captain, blue by now,
and took hold of her, as though to make her
keep still. I was pulling stroke, as I said
before. I pulled with my right hand and
dropped my left on the beggar's shoulder as
he leaned over towards the girl.

"Drop it," says I, "let her talk, *you* shut
up." Then I remembered it was the Lieutenant's business to chip in if any one's. "I
beg pardon, sir," says I, "but I forgot at
the minute."

"That 's all right, Bill," says he, cheerily,
"I was going to do the very same. Never
mind what the young lady says, captain,"
says he, "'t is a woman's privilege," and he
bowed and smiled at the girl. She never
looked at him, but she gave me a glance that
made me wonder what I 'd said to deserve
it. Sometimes I used to think she was frequent in a temper because she knew she
looked well that way. When we got to the
ship up she goes aboard, touching no one's
hand, spry as a kitten.

"Who 's the young lady?" says Captain Blakely, after he had got the Lieutenant's report and had said a few words to the brig's captain.

" She 's Nancy Barker of Plymouth, your honor," says the Englishman, " the daughter of an old shipmate of mine. The two were coming round from Yarmouth in the *Petrel*, a privateer in which John Barker had a share, sir, to Plymouth. John 's dead this week or more, and the rest of the lads aboard the *Petrel* hove me to and sent Nancy aboard, and then bore away God knows where. They left the lass on my hands and I 've been looking for the chance to put her aboard a homebound ship. The rest your honor knows," says he.

All this time Nancy, for as the brig captain says, 'twas her name, was looking all around very cool and staring at Captain Blakely and the other officers about as if she 'd like to know what they were doing aboard the *Wasp*. When the English skipper quit talking, of a sudden she speaks up.

"Yes, I 'm Nancy Barker," says she, "Gunner Nancy, they called me on the *Petrel* before I went aboard the brig yonder; for I can shoot a gun and aim it too," says she, " as your boat would have found this morning if this cowardly hulk," pointing at the brig captain, "had let me fire the carronade."

" Well," says Blakely very pleasant, " we owe you a good deal Captain," then he gave a few orders and walked aft. As he went I heard him say to the purser, " fit her up a berth somewhere well away from the fok's'le." Lord, you should have seen the girl's face for she heard him too.

" The farther the better !" she cried, "the farther the better. I 'd not suffer one of your beggarly Yankee swine to come near me," says she in a white heat. Then she stopped very sudden, ashamed I think of the talk she 'd used. She ran a few steps after Captain Blakely, and as he turned, saluted like a Jack tar and says quite low—"I ask your pardon, Captain," then turned

about and leaned against the bulwarks looking away towards the brig.

I liked her asking pardon, for I saw it
came hard, but she should ha' done it. No
decenter lot of lads ever came out of port
than we had aboard. Such as had n't wives
had sweethearts, except maybe Bill Fry, and
if I had n't one I was getting one so far as
my part went, pretty fast. If ever a man
was taken off of his feet of a sudden 't was
I. Says I to me before ever we came
aboard the *Wasp* with Nancy, "there 's the
lass I want." In my mind I ran her alongside of Lindy and she took the wind out of
Lindy's sails and left them flapping. 'T was
like a privateer alongside a Jersey coasting
schooner—and her spirit and her temper, I
liked 'em all.

"She 's not the sort to care for a swab
like Jim Downs, not for a minute," thinks I.
And this shows I did n't understand her any
more than any other woman. As I was
working upon a sail that wanted the needle,
I kept an eye her way. Once she looked

around and caught me and I could see she
remembered my face. They gave her a
cabin almost amidships that the purser's
clerk and Jim Downs had used, and stowed
them farther aft. I saw Jim come edging up
to her on deck, I guess 't was to show her
to her cabin. Says I to me, " now for sport.
She 'll keelhaul the little lubber if he stirs
her up," thinks I. Well he went to her and
bowed very polite and said something or
other and she half smiled at him and followed
him below like a lamb.

"Well," thinks I, "I guess there 's something in a ribbon shop or a church choir that
I don't understand about," and I picked myself up, for my job was done, shouldered her
little sea chest and walked below with it.
Jim was in my way as I came to the cabin
door.

"Out of the way mate," says I, " here 's
the lass's trunk."

" I 'll put it inside for the lady," says Jim,
very airy, and saying *lady* very hard ; to let
me know the way to speak to her, perhaps.

"Thankee," says I, "I carried it down and I 'll just set it inside for her."

She came to the door just then.

"Take the chest, Mr. Downs," says she, acting as if she did n't see me. Well I 'd naught else to do, so I handed the trunk to Jim and stood there a minute, awkward like, waiting I guess for a "thank you." She held out her hand to me and I took it for I thought she meant to shake hands. Blast me but she dropped a sixpenny bit into it.

When I 'm angry I 'm quicker to act and think than when I 'm in good humor, for then I 'm a bit lazy and slow.

"Thankee, Miss," says I, very stiff, "but you 've mistook me—I 'm an able seaman— *this* is the ship's boy—here you are Jimmy," and I took his hand, shoved the coin into it and shut it over it so hard he half cried out. Then I walked forward pretty sure I 'd done an all round smart thing and at the same time red hot at the girl's sauce.

By-and-bye I got cooler and then I saw I 'd passed on to Jim the insult meant for me

and that he 'd not deserved it more than I
had, and, too, that I 'd laid a heavy hand
on a little fellow, not man enough to clear
scores with me. Well, if I 'm wrong I 'll
say so. Back I went to the girl's cabin.
Jim was there yet, hanging round, helping
this way or that. I came up and put my
hand on his shoulder.

"Mate," says I, "a few minutes back I
miscalled you and put on you the cut that
was meant for me. I was wrong to do it—
't is no more your duty to fetch and carry
baggage than mine, and I ask your pardon,"
says I, red by now, and getting angry again
for the girl stood in the doorway looking at
us cool as you wish. Jim did n't speak up
at once but she did.

"Mr. Downs," says she, "he 's asking
your pardon and now I daresay he 'll be
wanting the sixpence back."

"Well, my man," she says to me, very
patronizing, "here it is again."

I was minded first to go about and have
no more to do with her, but of a sudden a

whim seized me. "I'll be even now," says
I to me, and I took the sixpence. "I'll
take it, Miss," says I, smiling, and looking
straight in her eye, "and as I see there's a
hole in it I'll wear it round my neck to remember you by. Many thanks to you,
Miss," says I, laughing as I turned and
walked forward again. After a few steps
I looked round. She caught my eye and
I was surprised she did n't look angry as I
thought she would. I guess I'd hit the
right way to deal with her but I did n't know
it then.

When I saw Jim Downs next I went up
to him. Somehow I felt more friendly
towards him than I had ever before. Now
this is a strange thing and a queer hitch
enough, that though I saw a man trying to
get the weather of the rest of us lads, me in
chief, with the lass, and hit as I surely was
by the first shot she fired, here was I actually
running alongside of him and being as civil
with him as if he'd been worth my powder.
And why? Just because I wanted to talk

with some one who talked with her. Just
because I thought in some way his knowing
her might help me too. I knew the fellow's
ways and that he 'd be thick with her before
long. For Jim had good looks, and a trim
little figure. He brushed his hair straight
up, and wore little whiskers like those he 'd
seen in a picture of Commodore Perry, and
he used to shift his light blue eyes in a way
that he thought brought him luck with
the girls. Then as I 've said, he 'd a sweet
voice.

"Well, Jim," says I, "what d' ye think
of the passenger?"

"Miss Barker?" says he.

"Yes."

"Why she 's a very sociable young lady,"
says Jim.

"I 'm glad you think so," says I, "for, tell
you the truth, mate, she struck me like a
little catamaran."

"I hope the boys won't annoy her," says
he, looking as if he thought it likely.

"No danger," says I, "don't fret yourself."

"Bill," says he, quickly, "you ain't a-going to wear that sixpence, are you?"

"Yes," I says, "that I am. It's good pay for the raking she gave me all for doing her a favor. Yes I am," says I, "what of it?"

"Oh, nothing," says he, "only she feels mighty bad about it, and thinks it might look as if, as if—"

"As if she really gave it to me for that use, hay!" says I, "Well, 't will serve her good and right. She'll know more next time than to be insulting a decent seaman," says I.

I was a little hot again, and of course when I cooled, I felt different. "Jim," says I, when I saw him next, "tell me what she said about that sixpence again." He told me. "Well," says I, "I'm going to give it back to her," and I started for the companionway.

"Hold on," says Jim, "better give it to me—she wont see you. Let me take it."

"Not if I know it," says I, "she shall

have it if she takes it herself, no other
way."

I started to go below when he ran after
me and caught me by the arm.

"Look here," says he, quite loud, hoping
to be heard by the officer of the deck, " don't
you go to annoying that girl."

"You go to blazes," says I, and slung my
arm round. He let go and as luck would
have it a roll of the ship sent him sprawling
into the scuppers.   I went on laughing.
When I got to the door of her cabin I stood
a minute, then knocked.   I felt a little
strange, and just a trifle the way I felt later,
when we went into action with the *Reindeer*.
She called out, " What is it, who 's there? "

" William Fry, Miss," says I, " with your
sixpence."

" What of it," says she very tart.

" Why," says I, " Jim Downs told me
you 'd been worrying for fear I 'd be wear-
ing it round like a token."

She laughed.

" Do you suppose any man would believe

I 'd give *you* or any other aboard this ship, 'a token,'" says she. "You must think pretty well of yourself Mr. William Fry," she says, and laughs again.

I took the sixpence and wedged it between the door and the jamb. "Here it is," says I, "keep it or leave it, 't is the last time I 'll put my nose in a way to be pinched." She said something else I could n't understand. I went away and as I went I heard the door open and shut. I stole back on tiptoe and the coin was gone.

I got on deck just in time to see the end of the brig *Neptune*. Everything that was of much value we brought aboard save the cargo, then set her afire. As our boat's crew came over the side and we stood away I heard some one curse near me, and saw the merchant captain looking at the burning craft. There were tears running down his face, and his mouth was full of the kind of word that I heard slip out. I did n't blame him. There was his ship gone to smoke and ashes with her cargo all aboard and he a prisoner. Just then at this minute the lookout sights another sail, and the *Neptune* was forgot by all of us in a minute.

One ship burnt, and another to chase and burn, perhaps a fight, or run for it ourselves, that 's what the life on a cruiser means, and as the sails were shook out and the breeze came fresher, and I lay out on the mizzen yards spreading the white canvas that always smells so good to me, I was glad I 'd shipped, and glad of life, and wanted no better, for the minute, than I had right there.

CHAPTER III.

HOW WE TOOK THE "REINDEER" BRIG-O'-WAR.

WE took the fresh sail we sighted and hardly had we laid her to, and thrown a crew into her, but another and another rose out of the sea against the sky line. 'T was like gunning in the old salt marshes down Biddeford way—a plover gets up right, then left, then just ahead, and you hardly know which to let drive at.

But we lost no time when once we singled out our bird. Three prizes we got in as many days and scuttled or burnt 'em all. I don't intend to keep log of our prizes except they be ships of war. I 've another journal home in Biddeford of my cruise along with Captain Porter and there 's nothing in it but yarns of the ships we hove to and

burnt or scuttled. This book is to tell of
another kind of work, and I only note the
ships we took, without saying more about
'em. I spoke of the *Neptune* because she
was our first haul and because of Nancy
Barker. Now for a different story.

'T was the 20th of June, and a gray day,
but very smooth. We were not far from
latitude 48°, longitude 11°, and were hot on
the track of two merchant ships that were
doing their best to get away. 'T was in the
early morning about four, when lookout
sings high and loud, and in a tone that
did n't mean more merchantmen:

"Sail ho! Sail on the weather beam!"

The captain was on deck. He 'd heard
the cry, and the tone in it, and up he comes
with his glass.

"Nor' nor' east, sir," says the boatswain's
mate to him, and I saw him level the glass
in that quarter. 'T was my watch on.
Presently he took the glass down and looked
at a midshipman, Mr. Geisinger, who stood
by. He was smiling, that pleasant smile he

had when pleased, and sure enough he was
pleased this time. He said something to
the middy, and then let him take the glass.
He looked, and handed it to the boatswain's
mate. In a few minutes the word came
forward that we 'd sighted one of the King's
ships this time, and not too big for us. So
all knew what that meant.

In a short time the news got below and
through the forecastle, and the men came
tumbling up.

" Where is she, Bill ? " they 'd call, and
" What does she look like ? " Old Josh was
pulled a dozen ways.

" Can you see her, Josh ? Is that her ? "

" No, you lubber, that 's a merchantman."

" Well, that 's her, then."

" A merchantman too, matey, where 's
your eyes ? "

" I see her, I see her; will she give us a
fight, d' ye think ? " and all that. The new
hands were excited, but I think not one of
them was scared. If one there was, his
name was Bill Fry, and he 'd seen a man's

head knocked into scraps by a round shot
once, and knew how such things looked.
Among the old hands there was n't so much
stir. They knew what a sea fight meant.
But I 'll not say one of them was scared.
They were not the kind. Very little shout
about 'em, not much brag, but " stand-bys "
all, who 'd swung cutlass and cleared away
with the boarders from the days we licked
the Tripolitan niggers, to this cloudy June
morning.

The captain was watching her every
minute and the day was breaking fast. Suddenly a sort of half cheer came from the quar-
terdeck, and soon we knew the cause. The
stranger was standing for us, coming right
down too as fast as the light breeze would
bring her. She 'd seen us, for her course
was changed of a sudden.

" Now, my lads," says old Josh, to a knot
of the green ones, " that 's the way with the
British navy. The quickest way to find out
who you be 's to come and see. She 's coming; and there 's some of you may wish you

was back to Portsmouth before two bells,"
says he. "They 're damn inquisitive," he
says, laughing, "those King's ships, and if
you don't play pretty sharp with your pikes
and cutlasses 't would be like their cursed
impudence to come right aboard, and be
pretty cross with you all."

We knew by his look that he did n't expect a call of the kind without our having
some say about it, and we were getting a
streak of John Bull's cocksureness ourselves.
We 'd heard a good deal of the *Constitution*,
and the *United States*, the *Hornet*, and the
first *Wasp*, and little enough of the *Argus*,
or the *Chesapeake*, and I guess there was n't
a man aboard, unless 't was Downs, and he
was only a man in a way of speaking,
who had a fear as to what would be the
upshot of the fight. And yet the breakfast
many of the men put in was light. Some
may say this is a mark of fear, but 't is nothing of the kind. It is a sort of excitement
and looking forward, as it were, to what is
going to call for all the nerve a man has got.

It 's the heart in a man working hard, and
the stomach can't be looked to be at its
best. With many a lad, too, '*t is* fear of a
certain kind, the kind that dreads lest he
will not play the man at the right time, and
that 's the worst fear of all.

One thing was pretty trying to the green
ones, that was the length of time the ships
took getting together. She had stood for
us soon as she made us out, and we 'd stood
for her; but the breeze was so light 't was
noon and later, before we began to get into
fighting distance.

I 'd forgot about Nancy Barker. She did n't
come on deck till along in the forenoon.
She had some acquaintances among the
crew of the *Neptune* to whom she talked.
Of course news got to the prisoners that we
were going to have a fight on our hands,
and there was plenty of excitement. Among
them now there was lots of unpleasant
feeling, but I could n't blame 'em. There
they were aboard of us, non-combatants, but
just as likely to stop a round shot or be

keeled over by a splinter as if they were n't
and by their own countrymen, too. 'T was
hard enough.

Nancy Barker, who by this time had got
pretty used to such of the men as naturally
came athwart her, was full of excitement,
but kept quiet. She had got into a way of
coming on deck and sitting by the main
hatch, with some kind of work in her hands
which she never worked on, but always carried. Old Josh said to her,—she treated
him decently, he was one of the few she 'd
talk to at all :

" Miss Nancy, you carry those signals to
fool folks," says he, "just as a ship-o'-war
hoists bunting to make a chase believe she 's
a merchantman," says Josh.

" D' ye think I 'm chasing you, you bloomin'
old flushinger ? " she 'd say, and he 'd laugh
fit to die. He and the other old lads made
a great pet of Nancy, but with the younger
men, except Downs, 't was nothing at all
she 'd say, or if anything, 't would be something that would make 'em wish she 'd kept

still. She was that nice to Downs that I
wanted a dozen times a day to drop him
astern for shark bait. And the little beggar
grew so cocky that I used to wonder he
did n't forget to salute his officers. But
I 'm going wide again.

'T was during the forenoon that Nancy
came on deck. She 'd got a glass, through
Jim, I guess, and began to examine the
stranger. He was getting close enough now
for us to see he was a brig-o'-war, carrying,
to all appearances, ten guns to the broadside. He could see us too, of course, and
what we were, but that did n't bother him a
bit. He could see we were more than his
weight, but perhaps he 'd been used to fighting Frenchmen, or had his head full of the
truck some English reports were loaded with,
about Yankee ships winning only by luck or
great odds, and that we were really cowards
after all.

Perhaps he was just pluck, and grit, and
sand, and was hunting for a fight. And I
guess that last is about the truth.

Nancy looked for a long time, then she turned to an old chap who stood by, and said : " I know her—and you 'd best turn tail while you can—'t is Captain Manners," she cried, giving way to her excitement, and laughing and catching her breath in half sobs, while the tears came into her eyes: " his crew 's called the pride of Plymouth, and I know many a man of 'em. Better tell your captain to get off while he can," she calls to old Josh, and then down she sits and cries.

Well, never a choke had been in her voice nor a tear in her eye all the days she 'd been aboard—in a trying place for a girl alone. She must have been as ignorant of what she 'd have to expect from us Yankees as the crew of the prize, who looked upon us as pirates in a way. But she never weak-ened, till this day, and then only when she saw her own flag and the ship she knew. They were tears, not because she thought her troubles, such as they were, were going to be ended, but because we were going to

see what a British ship-of-war could and
would do, and to be punished for our impudence.

I knew this, and I liked her the better.
Of course she had to go below in a few
minutes, for we had no room for women on
the deck just then. As she went, I passed
close to her. She used never to notice me,
though I felt sure she knew when I was
about. This time she looked my way, and
for my life I could n't help putting out my
hand.

"Won't you wish me good fortune?" I
says.

"The good fortune to see Plymouth jail
in a couple of days," says she, with a shot
out of her eyes.

"Well," says I, "if I do, you 'll may be
give me a sixpence now and then for grog,"
says I, not thinking at all of the coin she
gave me a few days before. I said it merely
to say something. She did n't seem angry,
and put her hand in the pocket of her dress
with a sort of smile. For a minute it seemed

as if she would say something pleasant. Then she turned and ran below.

"Good-bye," calls I, "if I happen to run foul of a round shot I 'll not trouble you nor Plymouth jail."

This was not all joke on my part. It cut me, why the Lord knows, to say good-bye to the lass who treated me like the deck under her feet. But I knew how thin your skull is against a round shot or grape no larger than a taw ally that boys use at school, and I did n't like to think I might not see that face (though it had given me but half a smile and that but once) when hands were piped to supper.

As I turned away, up she comes again in the companionway. She sort of signalled me, but I did n't heed it, half thinking I was mistaken, half that 't would mean another speech of the kind, the only kind she used to give me. I thought perhaps she was going to say something civil, for I 'd done her no harm but to admire her, which she knew I did. There was never a woman

quicker to see when a man admired her
than she was. But then I knew she could
be and would be pretty sharp tongued
and all for no reason at all. So I sheered
off.

All this is n't telling how we came into
action with the British brig. Keeping my
log as I did 't was hard to bar private doing
and thinking out of it; but all this occurred
while the two vessels were making towards
each other.

By now 't was an hour after noon and of
a sudden came a sound that took every
thought but one from the mind of each man
in the crew—the roll of the drum, beating to
quarters. I got to my place at my gun,
't was sixth gun of the port broadside and
a short time after, the *Wasp* went about and
stood dead ahead down upon the enemy to
get the weather of her. But the British captain knew his trade, and twenty minutes or
so later, tacked and stood away. Now Captain Blakely wanted the weathergage, and
the other wanted it too. It was a fine fight

of seamanship between 'em.   Not a gun was
fired, no long bowls played.   It was trying
to our new hands aboard, but they 'd been
trained too well to open their mouths.   About
half past two, the enemy tacked again and
came straight for us.   I could see that she
was taking in staysails and the boatswain's
whistle sent our boys aloft.

" She 'll weather us," says the gun-captain
to me, a minute or two later, " she 'll weather
us yet, no, by the Lord, we 're going about.
That 's seamanly, that 's right," says he half
under his breath.

You could hear the men at the gun breathing quick and deep but none spoke but the
gun-captain.   It was, I thought at the time,
the hardest half hour of my life.

" If fight is to come," thinks I, " God send
it quick."

But 't was not yet the time appointed.   As
we ran off with the wind on our port beam, it
seemed to some of the lads that we were
trying to get away; a low murmur came
from one or two of the guns, and then I

heard some officer's voice, sharp and deter-
mined but taut with excitement :

"Quiet, there, quiet, damn you—you 'll
get fight enough, quiet now."

Up went the flying jib on the British brig
and she began to creep up. It must have
pleased her to seem to be chasing a sloop of
war, yet from what I saw of her fighting, I
guess she 'd ha' chased a 74, if it had n't
waited for her. But we were n't worrying
to get away, not a bit. Suddenly, when she
was inside of a hundred yards from us, there
was a report, a swarm of grape and round
shot sang over the little stretch of sea between us, and crashed into our hull and
rattled about the shrouds and deck hamper.

There was never a sound on the whole
ship but the noise of a few bits of wood, a
rope end or two falling on deck; no man
stirred. The ships still kept their course
unchanged.

Again there came the boom of a gun, and
again the shot whistled about us. A man
at number ten gun gave a short, low cry, and

gripped his arm, and the blood ran down upon the white deck. There was a word or two from the officer of the section, the wounded man went below and a new man stood in his place.

Again came the report, they were working a shifting carronade on us, and not a gun could we train, running as we were, to answer; then again, and still there was not a brass mouth spoke for us. The men were red at the guns, not pale. Rage had got hold of 'em, and a mighty wish to talk back. At the fifth discharge of the carronade, which was well aimed and did damage, stoving in a boat, ripping and cutting the sails, and laying three men in the scuppers, I looked at the captain of the gun—'t was but a look, I said nothing, but he was savage at the delay.

"Shut up," he said, as though I 'd said a word, "we 'll fire on orders, not before!"

I heard the men at several guns curse to themselves, and many of them looked at their officers with eyes that fairly begged. But

not a gun nor pistol shot came from the
Wasp. She went on her course like a dumb
beast, when suddenly, for Blakely saw that
the enemy would not get upon his beam, our
helm was put a-lee, and we luffed. As our
guns began to bear, the order came to fire
from aft forward as the guns bore.

" Now, then, it 's our turn," yelled the captain of the first gun, and with a roar that
shook the ship, the firing ran along the port
side. Each crew yelled at the discharge,
and worked like devils at reloading. If it
was a long time waiting for the ship to get
to firing, 't was a lifetime to me from the
time number ten spoke up till 't was the turn
of six. The sweat fairly stood upon our
faces, the mouths of the men twitched, and
their eyes glared like cats'.

"Now," shouted the captain of our gun,
with a curse that he did n't know he spoke,
and old six let go her message.

" Load ! "—we loaded—" fire ! "—we fired ;
load and swab and fire, again and again,
God knows I can't tell much what went on

except by our gun, and 't was nothing but load and fire there. The ship shook with each broadside, and we saw nothing but smoke before us, with now and again dots of flame when the guns of the brig blew a passage through. They were fighting hard as we, may be harder, for our weight was heavier. We were creeping along in the light wind, closing nearer and nearer all the time. Ten minutes, they tell me, was all I lived till the first lull came—well, it might have been only one, or it might have been an hour—for I did n't seem to live, but only to be one of a lot of grimy devils, hauling, swabbing, lifting shot, and cursing; a crew out of hell.

Of a sudden, through the smoke, we saw the bows of the brig, splintered and riddled, her flying jib a bunch of ribbons, and all her ropes hanging loose. The two crafts were nearly touching when the enemy, with his helm a-weather, ran us aboard on the port quarter. We saw the boarders through the smoke run forwards, we saw our marines come hurrying aft. Some of the lads at the guns jumped to join them, and had to be fairly hauled back. The great moment was coming; 't was not gun for gun, but man to man, and it was hard to stand by our own work at the guns.

Under the bulwark the boarders were huddled, cutlasses drawn, and back of them our lads with the pikes. And now with a grating and grinding the vessels came together, and through the open ports, panting hard with excitement, and rage, choking with the foul-smelling smoke from the cannon, the two crews hacked and thrust and yelled.

Onto our bulwarks they came swarming, cutlasses rattled against cutlasses, pistols barked, and pikes pushed the foremost back, but not without pay for it, and not till the best of 'em were killed, or down.

'T was so near my gun I saw it all. I 'll never forget the look of those bull-dogs as they came aboard, and the devilish earnest way our lads went at them. 'T was bull-dog and bull-terrier, both much the same breed. They looked like us, they cursed like us, they fought like us, and if we *did* beat 'em off, we did n't follow 'em, or Lord knows we might a' had to eat the same pudding.

But they came back, they came back, though it must have been plain to 'em by now that we were too heavy for 'em and outnumbered 'em nearly three to two.

"Look there," shouted my gun captain suddenly, and there in the rigging, working his way to where he might board us, stood a man, in officer's uniform—his face pale and bloody, his hands that gripped his cutlass red and black as well, his smallclothes soaked in blood from a cruel shot in the thigh, and he staggered as he clutched the rigging; but game, game!

"Come on, lads, come on," he shouted, "once more and she 's ours!"

"Follow the Captain, huzzay!" yelled the men climbing up about him.

Then the Captain, for 't was Captain Manners himself, flung one hand to his

head and, with his sword still clenched in
his fist, fell back dead upon his own deck.
A ball from our mizzen-top had stopped the
life of as brave a man as I ever saw, bar
none.

'T was our turn now, and over the sides
we boys went. In a minute we were hot at
it on the *Reindeer's* deck. The British had
fallen back at their captain's death, but they
were of the right breed. Pistol, cutlass, and
pike all going hot, and the spatter and ping-
pang of the bullets from the top men dropping all around. But 't was not for long;
number, and good luck, yes, and clever
fighting, together was too much, and in a
few minutes the decks were cleared of all
who could stand, and the brig struck. And
who surrendered her? The Captain's clerk,
the highest officer left able to do so!

I 've but little to say of this fight beyond
what I saw of it. I was in it, one part of it,
and I know when I say 't was desperate hard
work I 'm telling no lie. We 'd eleven men
killed and fifteen wounded, the *Reindeer*

thirty-three killed and thirty-four wounded.
Her bulwarks, boats, and upper works were
wrecks. "Pride of Plymouth," I heard
again, her crew was called. Well, Plymouth
may well be proud of them, and all England
too, say I.

I was hurt a little myself—a splinter hit
me in the shoulder, knocking me down, but
doing little harm besides laming me for a
week or two. I went below as soon as the
brig struck, for I was dying for a drop of
water.

Out of her cabin amidships came Nancy
Barker and ran towards me.

"Well," says I to myself, "she 's glad to
see I 'm not hurt bad, I guess," but she
was n't thinking of me.

"Well," she cried, "so you 've struck at
last, have you?"

I stared.

"Of course you have, I tell you," she
almost screamed, stamping her foot—"the
fight 's over."

I was sorry for the lass. "Yes," says I,

gently as I could, "the fight 's over, Miss, but we have n't struck."

"I don't believe it," she cried, "I 'm going on deck to see."

I caught her by the arm—"'T is no place for you, Miss," I said, "and there 's danger, too, from falling ropes and halyards may-be——"

"I 'm going on deck," she said again and pulled away from me and ran up the hatch. Right across the top, dead and bloody, lay what had been poor Tim Stevens. She stopped, screamed, and almost fell back. I was close to her and helped her down.

"Go to your cabin, Miss," said I, "in God's name. 'T was your flag was struck, but your Plymouth lads fought the best men could, and if Captain Manners had lived "—I was going to lie a bit to comfort her, and say if the British Captain had lived the fight might have gone his way; but truth is 't was a lost fight, gallant as it was, from the first gun we fired.

"Captain Manners dead," says she, "and all his crew?"

"Not all," says I, "but a good half." She was very pale and quiet now and went back to her cabin. Thinks I, "she's got a sweetheart in that ship's crew."

Well, we burned the prize the next day— she was too cut up to keep—and we licked our own wounds, so to speak, and gave our own poor boys and the *Reindeer's* dead the sailor's burial they had earned.

To some folks the thought of slipping off a plank with a shroud of canvas and a shot at your feet is fearsome. But not to me. I've known seafaring men to die asking to be laid in a churchyard, under green grass. None o' that for me. I like the shark better than the worm, and clean green salt water is better to be mixed up with than the muck or loam of a village graveyard. Will I be the more forgot because there's no tombstone to me, nor no rhyme telling what a fine man I was and how I steered a straight course to heaven? Not I. Out of sight is out of mind whether you lie in the half acre about the meeting-house or drift with the currents of the salt sea.   And for me, let me have the same burial the two score brave lads from the *Reindeer* and *Wasp* got.   Side by side they went down into the ocean that they fought over, and that was proud of them ; and with them, commanding the dead, so to speak, went the body of Captain William Manners.

CHAPTER IV.

THE WAYS OF NANCY BARKER.

I THOUGHT Nancy Barker had a sweetheart on the *Reindeer*, and I was right. Part right, that is. For I think she cared but little for him, while he seemed to be half crazy over her. He was a lad no more than eighteen, I should think, and from Plymouth way. Boy as he was he 'd seen a good bit of the world, and picked up tricks of the devil in this port or that.

He made me think of Jim Downs in some ways, only Jim's cussedness was the quiet kind, and this youngster's was more aboveboard. I 'll call him Joe, as that was the only name he went by.

Two days after the fight with the *Reindeer* he came up on deck. He 'd been hurt a little, that kept him quiet a while, but now

he was in shape again, and being a lad, the
Captain had let him go about more freely
than the other prisoners, whom we had to
guard carefully. We kept 'em in irons because 't was the safest thing. We could n't
keep a guard big enough to take care of 'em,
over 'em, and mind you we had the crews of
three prize ships aboard as well. Why, had
they got loose, they might have made no
end of trouble. We were kind to 'em, to
such as we could be kind to. Many of them
were surly dogs, good haters, I guess, and
't was the presence of such that made us
careful.

But it was no trick to see what kind of a
craft young Joe was, and we gave him plenty
of sea room, and so it came that he found
Nancy. She 'd been talking with some of
the prisoners who knew her, and she knew
well enough that Joe was aboard, but she
made no try to see him, indeed, rather kept
out of his way. But the second day, as I
said, after the fight, she ran upon him standing abaft the main hatch. He was smoking

a dirty cutty pipe, and as he saw her he
started so it fell from his hand to the deck
and broke. I was not far off. To speak the
truth I think Nancy was going to talk to
me when she ran upon Joe.

Well, he went right up to her and before
she could say avast he put his arm round
her and kissed her. I looked to see her cuff
him, but she was too angry for that. I
reckon she only cuffed people she cared to
have kiss her.

"Lookee, Joe," says she, very cool, "I 'm
no child any longer, though you may be ;
don't you dare touch me again—after smoking a nasty pipe anyhow—no, nor at all,
d' ye hear."

I was laughing to myself as much at the
mixed-up reason she had for not wanting
him to kiss her as at the boy's look of sulky
surprise, when the boatswain's mate passed
me and, pointing to the broken pipe and
spilled tobacco, says, " Have that mess
swabbed up," and goes on.

I steps up to Joe. " Mate," says I, " just

redd up your muss there, it 's not ship-
shape."

"All in good time," says he, very saucy,
" I 'm talking to a lady now——"

" Must you always be interfering, indeed?" says Nancy to me very supercilious.

"You clean it up *now*, my boy," says I,
dropping my hand on his shoulder, and paying no notice to her at all. " This is a ship-
o'-war you 're on, where there 's such a thing
as discipline."

" D' ye mean, mayhap, we had none
aboard the *Reindeer?*" says he, quite hot
and bristling up.

" Oh, come, come, come," says I, taking
him round the waist and lifting him over to
the hatchway, " you go and get a swab and
redd this deck up ; don't you try to fight ;
we settled all that two days ago."

Well, he swabbed the deck.

Nancy seemed to forget she 'd been angry
at him, and stooped down and picked up
bits of the pipe and hove 'em overboard and
called him poor Joe, who 'd been hurt, and

said some men did n't seem to know the difference between big and little.

"Why, Joe," says she, "when that big rough "—there she stopped; I guessed, as I stood near by making believe not to listen, she 'd call me a swab or a lubber, for she had the words pat and was none too nice tongued to use 'em; but she was going to do worse—"coward," she goes on, and then over the course again—"that big rough coward had hold of you it made me think of this top-heavy, blooming, disguised frigate and our little *Reindeer*," says she.

All this made me two points or three to windward of pretty blasted mad. She 'd called me a coward and, more than that, she 'd miscalled the ship. I came right over; if she wanted to get me alongside, she 'd run up the proper signal.

"I 'm about twice Joe's size," says I, trying to talk cool, "and you won't say we 're twice as big as the *Reindeer*—3 to 2 is how we 'd rate, I reckon, and that 's not such a thundering big difference, 'specially when

you remember we knocked her into match
sticks and laid out half her crew."

"Yankee brag," says Nancy.

" I 'm sorry, though, I touched you, lad,"
says I, "for you 've a lame arm ; well, so
have I, but the Lord did n't build you quite
the way he did me, and I 'm sorry I handled
you."

"Legs don't count," says he, sulky.

"You 're always apologizing for laying
hands on little men," says Nancy.

"Yes," I says, very cool, for I felt they
were evening up by what they said for any
bad temper I 'd shown. "Yes, I always
will too when I do it, I hope," says I, and
turned to go.

" Did you say legs don't count, Joe," says
Nancy very pleasant, "why ashore now, a
man could run fast on a pair of long legs
maybe."

"But being aboard ship and on duty by
my gun I could n't use 'em, I suppose," says
I, turning round and going back to her side.
"Well, Miss, hark to me. You 've miscalled

me and run foul of me now the last time.
The Lord knows I 've not meant to offend
you, but you 'll have no more chance to be
troubled by me, so here 's good day."

I was so hot I talked like a fool, I guess,
but I said my say and went about my work.
Pretty soon I heard her and Joe hard at it.
Her temper was none of the best, and maybe I stirred it, for she stood all around Joe
and raked him from every quarter. By and
by Jim Downs passed me. I knew where
he was bound, and pretty soon Joe goes by
from the other quarter. 'T was Jim's turn,
I suppose, and for a long time they talked,
and then Jim sang a bit in a low voice, and
she sang too. She had a nice, rather deep
voice, and they seemed to know the same
songs. I soon knew why, for my work—I
was doing a trick at painting a bit of the
bulwarks just forward the mizzen-shrouds—
brought me nearer them every few minutes.
"Yes," Jim says, "my mother was from
Bristol."

"I knew you must be English, at least

7

part," says Nancy. "There 's something about you that don't look Yankee." All this was meant for me.

"Let 's try another song," says Jim, " wish I had my accordeon here."

"You would n't be allowed to play it in this place if you had, Jim," says I, forgetting I was n't in the talk at all.

"Ho!" says Nancy, "that gentleman with the long legs is listening, Mr. Downs. Has he got long ears as well, I wonder." Jim says nothing—he knew when to keep his mouth shut—but she went on.

"Do you reckon we could sing a bit more or do you guess we could n't?" This all for me.

Then they sang a spell. Old Josh came up near 'em and some others, and by and by when they were through he sang a verse of his song, his favorite, about the *Constitution* and the *Guerrière*. He did it to tease Nancy, and she knew it and talked back very brisk to the old man.

"Did you ever hear of the *Shannon*,

Josh?" says she; she was very familiar
with him.

"Yes," says Josh, "she 's the 74 as took
the *Chesapeake*, 38.

Then Nancy, of course, forgets it 's all fooling and gets mad.

"'T was ship to ship of the same size,
every way," says she; "if there was odds
't was with you Yankees."

"How about the *Chesapeake's* crew," says
another, "half green hands and Englishmen
and a spice of Portugee swabs."

"Oh, don't tell me of green hands," says
she very scornful, "you told me yourself,
Josh Sewall, that green hands fight as well,
when it *comes* to fighting, as the old hands.
Why even such long-legged Johnny Raws as
that yonder with the paint-brush will stand
by their guns, for a while anyhow."

Of course she had to hit at me. When
she was going a bit free I was always right
in her course. This time old Josh spoke up
for me. Maybe he 'd seen how she kept
driving into me.

"I agree," says he, "green hands do, when they happen to be the right breed, as the *Chesapeake's* were *not;* not all of 'em, anyhow. Of course Bill Fry fought well and his gun captain 'll tell you not a man aboard ship fought steadier; cool and quick he was as any could be."

I sat there painting, never letting on I heard, but I was caught with a blasted strange feeling in my throat to hear Josh setting me right to her, and the water got into my lights.

Well, there 's nothing in all this, maybe, to give it room in my log, but it 's of a piece of what went on every day, till a week from the fight with the *Reindeer* we sighted L'Orient and ran into port for repairs.

There's little or nothing to say about Nancy during this week, but that she fooled with Joe a bit, then seemed to take up quite steady with Jim Downs.

Twice she asked me questions and twice I answered 'em without looking at her. And once I looked at her without her speaking to me or knowing it, and she turned and saw me. If ever a girl knew when a man was looking at her she was the one; if he was a young man, anyhow. I 'll bet old Josh might have looked at her an hour and she never turn round. When she caught me looking at her, she rattling on with Jim, she stopped a bit and I noticed that she let him do the talking for a spell.

As I said, she played a bit with Joe, and the boy was man enough to be pretty sore, when she sent him down the wind, for the other. He 'd forgot his hard feeling against me and would sometimes talk with me about her.

"She 's high and mighty now," says he, "for why? God knows! She 's the same Nancy Barker as I 've kissed a dozen times in her father's tavern, 'The Anchor.' He was a retired mariner, he was. But now, blast my eyes, I 've but had one kiss, an' that I stole,—they go to that psalm-singin' son of a Yankee," says he.

"Shut up," says I, "you 're talking to me."

"You be ——," says he. "No, not that, Bill, you 're not so bad, I mean you 're a seaman anyhow, and s' help me I 'd take you for an Englishman (he thought this would please me) but Downs is a duffer,—now you know it. I s'pose he gets the kisses now."

"Say," says I, "was she an honest girl in Plymouth?"

I was kind of anxious as I asked this. I don't know how I thought 't would make a difference to me.

"Honest enough," says he, "for she never had heart enough to be other. What 's the Captain, your captain, I mean, going to do with the lass?"

"Oh, ship her off with a load of you Britishers on the next prize we heave to, maybe."

He seemed satisfied with this. "I 'll have a chance with her for a while then," says he, grinning—"without that chuckle-headed tune-slinger. I 'll take some of the pride out of her; I 'll teach her to give the go-by to a British seaman for a putty-faced Yankee."

"Oh, shut up, shut up," says I, "and hark you, mate. You 'll speak of her as a lady while you 're aboard us. I 'll back her to stand you off when we part company."

We put many of our prisoners aboard a neutral vessel that we hove to, and the Captain was for putting Nancy aboard with them. I remember the scene when she refused to go. "I 'll go in irons, no other way," says she. "You took me out of the *Neptune*, now you can land me."

"But, lass," says Josh, for 't was he they sent to tell her the Captain's wish, "we 're bound to France."

"I don't care," says she, "I 'd rather be there than — Josh," she says, suddenly, "don't you see it 's no place, that Portugee ship, for a girl alone," she says, blushing. "Such a mixed ship's company as that? Now, with you Yankees I 'm—well," says she, getting very red—" somehow you are n't so rough as many of our own lads." I thought then of young Joe, who was one of those we 'd put aboard the cartel, and I saw, or I thought I saw, why she feared to leave us.

Well, Josh reported to the officer of the deck, and he told the Captain. The upshot was that she stayed aboard. Captain Blakely saw, maybe, the hard position the lass would be in, among a raft of seamen from a number of crews. And he had himself a young wife at home in Carolina.

At L'Orient she left us.

There were many seamen felt as bad as if they 'd really lost a friend. She never failed to say she hated Yankees, but old Josh would tell her 't was all gammon, and she 'd laugh as though she did n't mind what he said. Of course, she needed help when put ashore —some one to lug her chest, and do this and that. And of course 't was Jim Downs did it.

She looked at me when she said good-by to the younger lads, not offering to shake their hands that they 'd 'a' worked off, some of 'em, to please her, but I paid no attention. I 'd made my mind up to it that 't was Jim she liked, if she liked any one, and maybe not him. The surgeon, Dr. Clark, a good, kind, and brave man, had found a Danish Protestant minister's family, to take the girl till a chance came to send her properly home, and she had money, quite a stack of it, so 't was not hard to find a port for her.

Well, Jim took her chest on his shoulder and she tossed us good-by, as I said, and off they went.

"There 's a nice way to leave shipmates," says coxswain, laughing a little, but as if he did n't see anything funny in it.

"Little catamaran!" says I.

"Hay, Bill," says coxswain, "I thought you 'n' she was thick."

"Not we," says I.

"Well," says bow, "I 'm glad it ain't that young pup Joe," says he, "though if it 's Downs instead, 't is pup eat pup, six o' one and half dozen t'other," says he, "only maybe 't is *not* Downs. Listen, mates," he says, "I was splicing a rope on the fo'k'sle the night before we sent the cartel off with the prisoners aboard. 'T was just light enough

yet to see my work and I was set on finishing
it.   Up walks Miss and Joe.   I could n't
hear much they said till she got the red flag
up and her temper going.   Then she says,
' 'T aint you will do it, anyway,' says she.
Then he says something and she laughs kind
of airy and says, ' No, nor him,' and then he
cursed as the boy could, the rough-tongued
sea-pup, and says, ' Then '*t is* Long Legs after
all, by thunder ! ' "

This was a puzzle to me, for I knew who
" Long Legs " meant well enough, but 't was
hard to guess what the drift of the talk had
been.   The other lads knew nothing of the
name she clewed to me.

" So, mates," says bow, " here 's a toss up
between Bill and me, for we 've both long
legs, hay, old Biddeford rock-cod," says he,
and fetched me a little kick as he swung on
his oar.

" Vast there," says coxswain, and we were
soon alongside ship.

We lay near two months in L'Orient.   We
fitted the ship up in every way, where she 'd

been damaged, and got her into as fine shape as she ever was. Of course we got liberty to go about town a bit, and one of the first things I did was to go to the parade-ground to see the troops drill. We 'd heard of French soldiers for the last twenty years, and I wanted to see 'em. But they did n't seem to me to have much go to 'em. They seemed like whipped men, and I found out why. They did n't like the old figurehead the French, some of 'em, with English and Russian and German help, had set down on the throne. They wanted Bony back and small wonder.

The first day I watched 'em train I saw a trim-built girl looking at 'em too. She seemed to know most of 'em, and when they got a chance they 'd nod to her or speak a word.

As often as I 'd get an hour ashore I 'd go to the parade-ground to watch the soldiers, and this girl was there each time. One day I went with Josh. The old man spoke a kind of lingo that Munseer understood ; Josh *said* 't was French, and I says to him :

" Find out who the lass is."

Well, he goes right up to her, passes a
word or two of " How d' ye do," or " Fine
day," maybe, then begins to go ahead under
full sail, and she chips in pretty soon and
answers back to him, and they laugh and
talk and are very sociable. By and by
Josh comes back, gets me, and hauls me
over. He said a few words, and she curtseyed and smiled very pleasant, then Josh
and she began again.

While we were talking who heaves in sight
but Jim and Nancy. She was still waiting
for a fit chance to get across the Channel.
They pretended not to see Josh and me at
first, but I saw they—that is, Nancy, kept
edging our way slowly, and they came up
with us at last, as the French girl left us to
cross the ground to some soldiers who had
broke ranks and gathered in a knot. All this
time I had no idea who the girl was.

Josh had kept the lingo going, but I could
n't understand. Now Nancy comes up and
Jim.

"Well, Josh," says she, quite pleasant, giving him her hand, "who is your pretty friend?"

"Oh," says Josh, laughing, "it's a young lady who belonged to the army, just as you did to the navy before you deserted. She's been the vivandeer of the Tenth Regiment that's here now, in Bony's time, and now she's out of her job. Bill, here, asked me to introduce him, so of course I did."

"Oh," says she, looking at me very hard, "'t was Mr. William, was it, and how do you do these days?"

"Oh, all right," says I, "and much better for seeing you again."

Now I said this for sauce. I thought she was going to rake me, and I made up my mind to fire back. But what I said did n't seem to worry her. In fact, she acted as if she liked it.

"Why," says she, "you can say civil things, too, can't you, Mr. Bill?" as if 't was I had been anything but decent to her.

"Well, Miss," says I, "I can, I hope, and

if you 'll kindly furl the Mr., and just call me Bill, I 'll take it very kind."

"What did you say the girl was?" she asked Josh again, not answering me.

"A vivandeer," says Josh.

"And what may that be?"

"Why, one as goes along with the regiment and gives 'em a drink during the fight —a little Dutch courage, perhaps, or maybe only water," says Josh. "They wear a kind of uniform like the men."

"What, breeches?" says Jim.

"Something like, my hearty."

"It don't seem right nor decent," says Jim.

"Well," says I, "if they 've the pluck to go among the bullets to help the poor fellows who are down, I don't care if they *do* wear breeches," says I.

Nancy looked at me quite friendly. "Bill," says she, "you 're not such a fool as you might be," says she, then as she walked away with Jim, who looked as if he 'd said the wrong thing, she calls back:

"Seems to me I'd come and see old friends."

Old friends! 'T was an odd title to give for what she 'd been to me, but I allowed to go the first chance that came.

My shore leaves were not so frequent nor so long as I wished 'em to be after this. I used to wonder what kept Nancy in L'Orient all this time. Several times she might have gone home, direct to Plymouth too, but there she stayed. She lived in the Danish parson's family, and there was a daughter about her age who followed her about and seemed to like her. Nancy told Josh she was alone in the world since her father's death, and was minded to see it a bit. Our ship's doctor once in awhile would visit her and talk with her about what to do. Once he talked with me for a spell, of Jim Downs, what kind of a lad he was, and all that. I gave Downs as good a name as I could by a little lying. "He was sober and industrious, when he lived at home," I said, " and sang in a church choir, too," says I. I guessed

at the time he thought Jim was what kept
Nancy so long in port. That's what I
thought myself, and so did Jim.

Well, I saw the lass, maybe half a dozen
times before we sailed. She used to watch
the drills sometimes, and one day I saw her
talk a long time in her broken French which
she'd picked up, with the " vivandeer." This
was the last day I had shore leave. It happened Jim was not with her that day. I
learned why, later on. We had got to be
good friends, and she told me she'd been to
Bideford in England, that my town was
called for. We were talking of this and
that, I don't recall what, now, because I only
talked so I could have some reason to be by
her, and so long as I heard her voice I did n't
much mind what she said so it was friendly.
'T was true I was hard hit, but as for her I
did n't believe she cared a brass farthing for
me. At last I had to say something with
sense to it, that is, something to the point.

"It's time for me to be at the wharf,"
says I, "the coxswain 's not a good hand to

wait, and the third officer 's ashore, too, and
he 'll not wait, if coxswain *would*. I must
be saying good-by, Miss—Miss——"

"Nancy," says she, in a queer voice.

"Yes, Miss Nancy," says I, thinking she
was prompting me, "maybe we may meet
some time again."

"'T aint likely," says she, looking at me in
a way I could n't understand. "Maybe
you 'll be ashore to-morrow again—if you
don't sail till day after?"

"No," says I, "'t is the last leave I 'll get.
There will be some ashore to-morrow to get
supplies and more water, but that 's in the
purser's line. He 'll have Jim ashore, likely,"
says I, looking at her very close.

"Indeed," she says, very lofty, and it
made me feel uncomfortable. I 'm not
altogether a fool about women, and I know
when a man 's been keeping steady company
with a girl like Nancy, and suddenly when
it comes time to part, she acts so haughty,
it means most generally that he 's not come
up to time, as the saying is, and thinks I,

"she 's angry with the lad and maybe willing to be civil to you, Bill, but don't you be a fool, mate."

So says I, "Yes, Jim 'll be ashore, and—and—yes, he 'll be ashore," says I, quite red, for I reckon 't was harder for me to hold my luff than I thought, "and good-by, Miss——"

"Nancy," she says again, and looking half vexed and half amused, and if so there could be another half, half sorry—"Miss Nancy," says I, again, though I saw no reason for her to be prompting me, and took her hand and she gave me a good grip like the brave girl she was, and I left her.

CHAPTER V.

NEXT day of course there were men
ashore getting water, getting supplies
of the kind that you must have fresh and
can't stow away a week ahead of sailing; and
as I guessed, Jim was ashore most o' the day.
'T was dark when the last boat came out,
crowded with seamen and baskets of fresh
vegetables and several casks of water.

Jim was aboard by then. He had n't
stayed till the last boat and it riled me to see
him waste time he might have had on shore,
lying round the ship, for he did nothing but
sit about and look sulky. And he might ha'
been seeing Nancy, and would ha' been, had
he been a man, thinks I. At last I up to
him and says:

115

"Jim, if I 'd been you, I 'd been saying good-by to that pretty little craft over in the town that you 've been convoying so much lately."

"You mind your business, Bill."

"Well, well, mate, don't be so cocky. I meant no offence—but—'t is truth I tell you, I think she was expecting something of the kind."

"What do you mean," says he, looking at me close—"you 're trying to crow over me," says he, very low, "but damn you, big as you are I won't take it."

Well, of all wrong-headed sea calves! "See here, mate," says I, "I meant friendly, and there 's the end. I don't understand your signals and you can't read mine, so let 's stand away," and with that I left him. What he meant, to save my life I could n't tell. And 't was just about then that the last boat's crew came climbing over the side.

Next day we sailed, and oh 't was good to be off once more. If the cruise was exciting before, it was doubly so now. For we knew that John was looking for us, and his bull-dogs would be on the watch. But we knew our ship and the speed that was in her, and we knew our crew and the handiness of them and the Captain's cool nerve and pluck; and speed, and skill, and spirit man a cruiser as it should be manned.

We 'd taken a few new men in port, from a couple of privateers that lay there. Good keen fellows they were too, but with their noses in the wind for Indiamen all the time. Lots of fight in 'em, but greedy dogs. 'T was one of these, the second day after sailing, suddenly shouts out:

"Here 's a stowaway by thunder, and a lass too," and a half dozen men ran to the spot.

Back from behind some bales and barrels in the waist of the ship who comes out, pale and covered with dust, with her hair fallen down her back, dressed in a kind of boy's togs, but Nancy Barker!

'T was a strange sight—I never saw the like. The men were nonplussed—some laughed a little, then eyed each other, then looked at me, or for some one else. Josh goes right up to her, and she put her head on his shoulder and sobbed.

"Room here, lads," says the old man, looking round, "give the lass air and leave us two."

The men drew away pretty quiet—they seemed to think there was something in the wind. 'T was not old Josh the poor girl had followed off to sea, and I said to myself, "if there's harm been done, I'll wring Jim's neck on the chance of being right, if I'm run to the yard-arm for it." And some of the men, the older ones, gave me strange looks as I went by to the deck.

What the lass told Josh I did n't hear but half of, not till long after. The officer of the deck heard what was going, at once, and ordered the lass on deck, but the boatswain says a word in his ear, and he listened, looking very grave and angry, and then says he:

"Have the lass and Sewall, and Downs,

and Fry to the ward-room at eight bells," says
he. Boatswain passed the word to me and
by and by to Josh when he came on deck.

I went up to him and he took me by the
arm. Says he, " Bill, you 're a good lad, but
what a fool you always was," says he.

" Well," says I, " what 's this to do with
Nancy being aboard the *Wasp ?*"

" Well," he says, " nothing that I know of,"
and then he laughs. I was glad to hear him
laugh, for I knew then no harm had been
done, so far as he could know. " Well,"
says I, " you and me and Jim Downs and
Nancy go to court this afternoon."

" So be it," says he, " you 'll hear a funny
story then, mate."

Well, at eight bells in we go to the ward-
room. Nancy, who had been put in her old
cabin, still wore her boy's rig. 'T was not
exactly a boy's rig ; 't was breeches and
skirt, jacket and cap ; the skirt came to the
knees like a long coat. She was still pale,
but Lord bless me she had had only a drop
to drink and a bite since she came aboard,

and small wonder she looked white. But she had her spirit back again, and had got herself up with a ribbon to her collar, and spoke to Jim, and paid little attention to me, just like old times.

In the ward-room was the Captain, very grave, and with him the Chaplain, the Surgeon, and Mr. Tillinghast, who was officer of the deck when Nancy was found, and Mr. Baury, the third officer.

" When did you come aboard ? " says the Captain, slowly, looking at Nancy in a sort of pitying way.

" Last night, your honor."

" On the last boat ? "

" Yes, sir."

" Mr. Baury, you were with that boat ? "

" I was, Captain."

" How could this girl get aboard without your seeing her ? "

" Well, sir, 't was dark and the boat was full of bales and baggage. She is in men's clothes, in a fashion, and I daresay she was hid in the boat before I came aboard."

"I was, your honor," says Nancy, quite simple like.

"You wait till the Captain asks you questions, lass," says old Josh.

"What was your reason for coming aboard?" says the Chaplain.

"One minute," says Captain Blakely, and leaned over and said something to him. They both seemed troubled and embarrassed, and presently the Chaplain asked her a different question.

"Have you any complaint against any of the crew, Miss Nancy?"

"Ah," thinks I, "he has come to it." She spoke up very bold and firm and looked him in the eye.

"No, sir," she says, short and proud.

"Well," says the Captain, smiling, and sitting back as if a load was off his heart, "why did you come aboard, my lass? This is no place for women. We're not a packet ship, but a cruiser. I can't be running into port to land you again, and it may be weeks before I can put you aboard a vessel bound to your own home."

Nancy hung her head and seemed a bit taken aback. Then suddenly Josh pulled his fore top-knot and says:

" If you please, Captain, the lass, because I guess I 'm old enough to be her grandad, has told me somewhat about why she came aboard, if so be I may speak my knowledge about it to your honor."

"Go on, Josh," says the Captain, good naturedly.

" Well, sir, it 's this way.   She used to see the vivandeer——— "

" The what ? " says the Captain.

" The vivandeer, sir; the lass as carries the brandy and stingo about for the Frenchmen in their marches and fights."

" The *vivan de yare*," says the Surgeon back of his hand to Captain.

" Well, sir, she 's naturally fond of the sea, and she 'd got used to the *Wasp*, and knew she was a fighter, and had a top-rate set of officers, including chaplain and surgeon," says Josh, who was as sly as an Irishman and always a hand to joke.

They were all laughing by this time. The
old man was a kind of pet aboard himself.

"So," says Josh, "she guessed she'd come
aboard and sign as 'vivandeer,' and so she
got her uniform and just came aboard. And
that's the yarn, please your honors."

"But," says the Surgeon, trying to look
sober, "what's your people to do at home?"

"I'm alone in the world," says she, very
simple.

"But," says the Surgeon again, "you'll be
fighting against your own home."

"I'll do no fighting," says she. "'T is
not fighting to give lads their grog and pass
'em a cup of water in action, surely. And
then you're like my people, too," says she.
"I thought once Yankees were all niggers,
or yellow men, or red Indians, but you look
like Englishmen, and there's some of you
with Devon names too," says she.

Well, every one laughed at this, and we
were all dismissed but Josh. He knew something that he did n't tell us, and I made up
my mind he was kept to be questioned

further.   I overheard the Surgeon and Chaplain talking, later that day, as I was aft on duty, and one says, " That 's the man " ;— whom he meant I did n't know.   Then Chaplain says a little later, " But she 's an odd pet to have aboard," and Doctor says, " As safe with this ship's company as if she were at home."   And I knew they were talking, then, of Nancy Barker.

Jim Downs all the time we were before the Captain, had hung his head as if he did n't care what was said or what came, but when Josh said the girl wanted to be a vivandeer and she backed it up in the way she did, he looked sort of surprised, and then seemed to cheer up a good deal.   When we all went forward again he and Nancy struck up just as if nothing had happened.

Josh came forward pretty soon, and he got such men as he could about and made a little speech.   Says he :

" Messmates, Nancy Barker has calculated to ship with us as a ' vivandeer.' "

" Say it again, Josh."

"Hold your jaw, Ben. You know what I mean—the lass who gets their grog for the lads in action, same as the Frenchmen have, or used to have, anyway, in their regiments. Now she's as honest a girl as lives, and whoever says no, or acts toward her as if she wa' n't, has got to lick Josh Sewall——"

Here the crowd stamped and clapped— "Or Bill Fry—hay, Bill?"

"Why yes, mate, of course," says I.

The crowd stamped again. "And Jim Downs," says Josh, with a wink, and the crowd fairly yelled.

"Maybe," Josh went on, "she won't find much occupation, as the office of 'vivandeer' ain't been much as yet in the American navy, but I presume she will help in her way. Maybe," says the old man with a chuckle, "she can be a mother to you younger ones, a sister to some—and," suddenly getting quite hot, "she 'll be a daughter to me, and every mother's son of you will treat her as if she were, by the Lord. She makes but one cruise with us, for the

Captain thinks she must go ashore when we get home, and maybe she 'll adopt the country, and maybe she 'll annex one of Columbia's son's."

He winked at me when he said this, and some of the lads laughed. I could n't understand the old man's ways, and I did n't understand him when he clapped me over the back, as he got off the keg he'd been standing on, and says : " Billy, my boy, you 're a comfort to your mother, I guess not, but you don't know beans with the bag wide open," says he.

" Lookee here, mate," says I, " you 're too old to be running free across me that way," says I, and he laughed again, like to split.

All next day I did my best to get alongside Nancy, but 't was no use. She was n't just as short and peppery with me as she was at first, but 't was " stand off and don't come too close," in her way of acting.

It seemed to me, when she said good-by in L'Orient, that she was sorry to see the last of me, yet now when she was where she

could see me every day she did n't care a
ship's biscuit for my company. So the
fourth day out of port, I kept my distance
and dropped back on my plan of not speaking to her. She reminded me of some
skippers I 'd seen, mighty nice to you till
you shipped and went aboard, and tartars
once they got you in the fo'k'sle. "She
shan't stand off and on this way with you
any longer, Bill," says I to me, and so I kept
my course and gave her sea room.

Well, she did n't like that. She could n't
see how I could let her alone, I suppose, and
wanted to find out. So by and by she comes
up to me.

"How did you like me in the vivandeyare
dress?" says she. She 'd got another kind
rigged up by this time.

"Well," says I, "I can't rightly say that I
liked you in it; 't is well enough for a French
girl maybe, but to come among a ship's crew
of Americans, why—"

"Why, it shocks you I suppose," says she,
laughing.

"Well, yes," says I, "I can't say it does n't,—you see, we 're not used to that at home."

"Tell me about where you live," says she, suddenly jumping onto the bulwarks, by the foreshrouds, and paying no attention to what I 'd been saying, though I thought 't would anger her maybe.

"Why," says I, "'t is a town, as you know, called Biddeford."

"Oh, blast the town," says she in her free way, "tell me about your home — any sisters?"

"One," says I, "married, and gone away from home."

"Well, that 's good," says she—I stared, and she blushed suddenly all across her face.

"I mean that 's good—it 's right for a girl to marry if she gets a good husband, aint it, Will?" says she.

'T was the first time she 'd called me that name, and I liked the ring of it. "Well, yes, I guess so," says I.

"Do you only guess," says she, "can't you ever be sure, I wonder?"

I laughed at her—she was so saucy and trim sitting there on the bulwarks. "Well," says I——

"Do you ever open your mouth without dropping out a well," says she, laughing at me.

"Well——"

"There you go again."

"Miss," says I, "do you want me to answer questions you put to me or to just stand here and fool?" says I, half pleased and half riled.

"What question did I ask?"

"Why, if it wa' n't right for a lass to marry if so be she gets the right man?"

"I remember now—What 's your answer?"

"I say yes, but I say she does n't always get the right man."

"Then it 's his fault, perhaps," eying me very close.

I did n't suppose there was anything in the wind; it seemed to me that she was just

9

using up her time by taking mine, and rattling away at no target at all. So I says:

" No, not the man's fault that I can see," says I. " She might be just the wrong girl for the right man, maybe, and you can't blame him for sheering off or running away," says I.

She got very red and was quiet a minute. Then she says slowly :

" Tell me, do you think I came aboard to, to follow Jim Downs? " She was very red and would n't look me in the face.

" Why, no," says I, slowly—" I, I guess not, I——"

" D' you mean to guess about that," she cried, very angry and looking now right into my lights. " Don't you guess about such things, you thick-headed Yankee," she says. " I 've wasted time enough on you, God knows. The only man that is a man in the ship's crew is Josh," she says; " he 's got head, and heart, and aint all arms and legs and blasted guess-work," she says, falling into rough language, which she always did

when angry. " And you think I 'd follow—
Oh, I 've no more time to waste on you,"
says she, almost crying, and jumps down and
walks away.

I was too surprised and flustered to do
much more than go on splicing the rope I
was at. " Well, well," thinks I, " if she
was n't following Jim who was she?" And
she would n't ha' been so angry if he had n't
had something to do in the matter. But
there 's one thing I don't believe," says I to
me, " and that is that there 's anything wrong
between the two—She 's honest is Nancy—
if any girl I ever saw was—I 'll talk to old
Josh," thinks I, " and take a few soundings
so I shan't go aground with the lass again as
I did just now. Maybe I 'm a blasted fool,"
says I to me. Just why I felt that way I
can't say for my life. But I was beginning
to get the feeling on me.

I 'd a good enough opinion of myself. I
was a tall figure of a man, with good teeth, I
did n't chew, and a plenty of light hair and
blue eyes. Lindy seemed to like me and it

did n't seem strange to me. But that was because I did n't care so very much, I guess, for Lindy. Now I 'd a been willing to give a hand for this girl Nancy, if I had n't kept myself down by telling myself 't was no use, and getting help in the job by the way she treated me. And as I felt so for her, so it seemed to me that it would be impossible for her to care for me. I was the sort that looks on the dark side of things in which his heart is 'listed, and that 's the whole story.

As I sat pretty glum and quiet, puttering away at my job, by comes Nancy again. She carried her head high and came along like a breeze. She was n't going to notice me, but I got up and touched my cap——

" Excuse me, Miss," says I, " but I want to say that I don't think there 's anything wrong between you and Jim Downs and I 'll lick the swab who dares think so, out loud," says I, " or to himself, if I know of it."

She looked at me in a strange way—I was going to say my little speech over again, thinking she had n't understood me, when she blushed, leaned against the side of the ship, and put her hand to her throat.

" Do you mean to say that any one dares think so," she says at last quite low.

" Why," says I, " 't would not be very strange maybe."

" My God !" says she, " it never came to my mind till now."

She looked over the side of the ship and I could see her sobbing. I could n't stand that and I went up to her. " Miss Nancy," says I, and she turned on me——

" So you don't believe there was anything wrong," says she laughing, though her eyes were full of tears, " well, you 're a good charitable soul, Mr. Will," says she, " but don't bother to be championing me," says she, " I 'll look after my own good name. Still I 'm obliged to you," says she, " for your good opinion." So she tacked and stood off and left me, sure I 'd made things worse than before for Bill Fry.

As soon as I got the chance I ran along-side Josh.

"Josh," I says, "Nancy talks to you as if you were a sort of guardeen—Now can you tell me why she always gets on my weather quarter and fires into me? Is it anything I've done?"

"Nothing you've done," says the old bird, laughing, "mebbe something you've left undone," says he.

"Talk plain, matey," says I, "what's in the wind?"

"Your sails, you lubber," says he, as if he were half angry, "your sails, a-flapping; what have you been saying to her this morning?"

I told him what I said and he all but took me by the collar. "You damn thick-head," says he—"So you had to insult her as well as——"

"Come now, Josh," I says, "none of that talk."

"You hear me out," says he, very angry— "I'll tell you something, you blind sculpin."

"Don't call names," says I.

"I'll call you all I want," says he, "and

you 'll take 'em, for by the Lord Harry
you 've earned 'em all—Listen to me, you,
Bill Fry—I 'm going to tell you what I 've
no right to, maybe, but blast me I can't let
things snarl up this way. If you can't see
things yourself I 'll be your eyes," says he,
very hot.

"Well, go on when you get your breath,"
says I, cool, but angry by now, and he looked
at me and wagged his head.

"Oh, Bill, Bill," he says, and laughs of a
sudden, "you 'll be the death of me."

"Look here, Josh," says I, "get your jaw
tackle running to rights, mate, I 've no time
to stand here all the morning."

"You 're mad now," says Josh, "as I
meant you should be, for Bill, when you 're
mad your brain clears up a bit. You 're too
lazy to think much when you 're in good
humor, my lad, my lad—that 's the fact.
Now just keep it up, you dull hearted skate,
that 's right, keep mad, I want you to; but
listen——"

What Josh was going to say I did n't

know, but just as he said " listen," as if it were what he meant, lookout sang high and clear : " Sail ho—sail ho—sail on the weather quarter." Then in a moment, " Sail ho, sail ho, sail dead ahead."

Of course every one was looking alive at once, and sure enough, off to our weather quarter, to the weather beam and almost due ahead were sails. Why, 't was a fleet. Every man was alert again with the old spirit. We were game to fight or make prizes, come whichever luck was to be.

In two hours we found it was not to be our fortune to make the string of prizes we thought we should, and not to fight either. 'T was a convoy of ten sail, and the convoy was a 74-gun ship. And yet Captain Blakely, like the man he was, made chase.

CHAPTER VI.

HOW WE TEASED THE "ARMADA" AND SUNK THE "AVON."

WHEN I say made chase of course I don't mean that he intended getting too close to the 74, which we afterwards found was the *Armada*. But he meant to hang about the convoy and pick out a fat prize if the chance befell.

I 've watched a butcher's dog, 't was a brindled terrier I recollect, pick a cow out of a lot of cattle with an old bull at their head. For some time they stood him off, huddling up in a crowd with their bows towards him, and then the bull would come charging around and drive the pup off. But he stuck to it, and kept chivvying and worrying, till by and by he cuts out a heifer and off they go. When he 'd got her far enough out the

drove he 'd pin her by the nose till his
master came up.   And this is what Captain
Blakely did with the merchant fleet.

Lying off to windward and astern, he 'd
edge up and up, then of a sudden clap on
canvas, and stand for the nearest sail; and
she 'd run for the nighest her and the two
would crowd for the next; then the big
hulking 74, with her three rows of teeth
showing, would put her helm down and come
for us, and when she got almost near enough
to chuck a round shot onto us, about ship
and away we 'd go.

This was sport, and there was no danger
to it.   'T was fine practice in seamanship.
and had plenty of healthy excitement about
it without letting you fear you might be
expected to digest a grapeshot for dinner.
The men were gathered in groups about the
forecastle, such as were n't standing by to
jump aloft or handle the ropes. We were
pretty busy watching the fun, and yet had
some time for yarning as well.

While we were beating up towards the

fleet after having been run off by the line-o'-
battle ship for the third time, coming up
easy, so as to let the flock scatter, Nancy
comes on deck and stood by the main halyards for a minute, watching the game. She
looked very handsome as she leaned against
the rail, her skirts shaking in the wind at
times, and at times caught about her. She
had a sailor's cap on, so rigged that her long
hair was held inside it, but a curl or two had
fallen outside. I guess she knew how, for
't was hanging down when she came on deck,
and the wind aint apt to be very high below
hatches. She wore a bright blue ribbon at
her throat; *that* I noticed specially, as it
used to be a red one. But "she was going
to adopt us," Josh said, and was learning our
bunting.

Well, there were some six or eight of us
lying together just abaft the capstan, and we
quit looking at the merchantman and their
"guardeen" to look at Nancy. Presently one
of the men we'd got from the privateer, a
son of a Portugee swab from New Bedford,

where there's a nest of the yellow beggars, says something in his nasty, foreign way—I did n't hear what it was, but I saw Jim Downs draw off and hit him a wipe with the flat of his hand. Up springs the Portugee, twice the man Jim was, and in a minute he had him by the throat.

Nancy screamed and ran below.

I like a fair tussle at times, tho' a man-o'-war's deck 's no place for it between men of the same crew, but 't was an officer's business to interfere, and I would n't ha' spoiled sport except that 't was no fair fight—little spindly Jim and the thick-built bull-necked Portugee. I just took him by the neck and pulled at him till he came off. While I held him, Jim, half choked, says, panting hard: " He said she was—— "

I aint going to put down what it was, but I got a better hold on him and slung him across the deck. " There," says I, " you dirty, yellow swab ; 't is lucky Jim's hand hit you, not mine. Jim," says I, clapping him on the back, " you 're a better man than I

gave'you credit for; here's my hand, though
we aint been very good friends. Well," for
he did n't take it, "all right, mate; 't is a
pity for a man with pluck to have malice,
too, but—— "

Just here I heard a yell from a couple of
the lads, and saw them run towards me, and
at the same time a feeling as if I'd been burnt
ran along my ribs. Before I could do more
than rip out a word, the men were tumbling
around the deck atop the Portugee, Pico;
that was the name he went by. Well, another
went behind me and hauled the beggar's
knife out of my jacket. I could feel the
warm blood trickle down my leg, but I knew
in a minute 't was only a scratch. The officer
of the deck, of course, was on the spot right
off, though he had n't seen the first of the
shindy, owing to the bigger attraction of the
chase. Pico was ironed and put away in
the brig to cool off, and I went aft to the
surgeon.

I stripped off my jacket and shirt and he
put a bit of plaster on the cut, and asked me

how 't was it came about. I told him, and
gave Jim a good word, for the man's sudden
spirit pleased me, in spite of his sulky ways.

"Well, Bill," says the doctor, "you must
lookout for this precious hide of yours;
you 've got too much depending on you."
I laughed.

"Not I, Doctor," says I.

"What," says he, laughing, and looking at
me very sly, "no wife?"

"Not I, Doctor," says I, laughing hearty
now. "Nor my mother aint a poor widow
woman neither, for dad 's good for twenty
year yet, and I 've a brother at home as well."

"You 're very independent, then," says he,
cutting a slip of plaster and laying it on
lengthwise the cut.

"Yes, sir," says I.

"No sweetheart?" he says, taking another
side-shot at me out of his lights.

"No, sir," says I, very quiet, for I 'd given
up any thought of Lindy, and gave up easy,
too.

"Well," says he, "now there 's that pretty,

trim, little privateer, the *Nancy Barker*, she's going to settle in America. What do you think of her, now?"

Well, I guess I turned pretty red, not all because I was flustered, but part because I did n't allow 't was Doctor's business. Still I had to answer respectful.

"Well, sir," says I, a-buttoning up my jacket, "she aint been cruising in my latitude and longitude," says I, using the kind of talk he 'd been slingin', "and I guess she 's been cut out already."

"Who 's done it?" says he, as he stood by the door to show me out.

"Well, sir, Jim Downs, if you ask me," says I; "leastwise that 's my guess."

"You 're a damn fool, Bill," says he, sort of dry, and opened the door.

There aint much to do if your officer calls you names but get out of his course, particularly if you have a temper that makes you itch to talk back, so I went back to the steerage and then on deck. I got there just in time for fun, and for a spell I forgot what

had just happened and what was like to set
me thinking. For some cause, maybe she
was n't so fast as the others, maybe she was
heavier loaded ; but, whatever 't was, one of
the convoy had fallen behind the others and
was steadily dropping astern. The Captain
had seen her from the first. He had his
eyes on her, and without steering so that
't was plain what his purpose was, he kept
the ship well in hand so as to stand down
upon her at the right time. We were so
speedy that we could keep to leeward of
the fleet and yet reach them handily. Suddenly we went about and beat up into the
wind straight for the lagging merchant-ship.
How they ran up aloft aboard her ; men
swarmed out on the yards, and her extra
canvas was shaken out. She was sure we
were after her, as we were, but not just
then. And pretty soon down from the lee
of the fleet, where we 'd drawn her by lying
to leeward, comes the 74 with her big-bellied
bow, carrying a bone in her teeth, like some
overfed yard dog. She let go a couple of

bow-chasers at us when she thought the
range was anywheres near right, and they
fell half a mile short.

John's gunners, barring the men aboard
the *Shannon*, and one or two other crack
ships, were n't worth the powder they
burned. British seamen could fight at close
quarters as well as we could, but they could
n't shoot, barring Brook's men and Manners's. We paid no heed to them, but beat
steady up the wind. When we got near the
ship we 'd singled out, we saw them throwing a lot of cargo over the sides, brass guns
and gun-carriages, by thunder, and we knew
't was a valuable prize to make.

Meantime the *Armada* was coming up to
the merchantman from the lee quarter, and
we were about a half mile under her stern.
I looked to see the Captain make a dash at
her, for the 74 was still a good two miles
away. But 't would have been a foolish risk,
and he knew his business. On we went up
into the weather quarter, and the men began
to think we were going to give the job up, at

10

least so far as this particular ship went. And now the 74 herself acted a bit as if she thought so too. We 'd seen seamen aloft busy at the flying sails, as if she were crowding on all canvas to head us off, and now they began coming below like she 'd given up the notion; and as we got well to stern and weather of the last craft, we saw her luff as if she 'd got an idea.

Now the two leading sails were faster than the others and had drawn well ahead. Suddenly Captain Blakely, having got good sea room to the weatherward, comes about and stands in the direction of the two leaders, with a good breeze on his port quarter and the 74 lured down to the tail of the fleet. Half the men aboard the *Wasp* thought 't was the game to cut the two ships out before the *Armada* could get into distance to protect 'em. The Captain of the 74 was sure of it. About he goes and crowds on up to starboard of the fleet, expecting to meet us round in front of the convoy maybe, but right there he made a false reckoning.

All of a moment the *Wasp* went about, the boatswain's whistle sent us aloft, every sail we carried was shaken out, and instead of running S. S. W. we bore down N. N. W., straight on the ship we 'd singled out at first.

Lord, how we flew—'t was a fine breeze and we went right ahead of it. The poor merchantman did n't seem to have the life left to run. There was no use. We were almost alongside before the great lubberly line-of-battle ship had got about and fairly headed for us. We luffed, and at the order a boat was lowered away and a crew sent aboard the prize, and in a minute after our boys had climbed aboard, her helm went up and she stood away in company with us. We ran off nor' nor' west across the bows of the *Armada*, who wore and gave us a half broadside that went wide and high. Old Gridiron flapped from the spanker gaff, looking wide-awake and merry, as the old bunting somehow always looks, to me anyhow; and I swear this day it seemed to wear a broad smile across its stripes. Well, we tried the trick again, but this time they knew the catch, and content with what we 'd got we went on our course.

By two bells we were 'way to leeward of the convoy ; by four they were out of sight.

Life was dull aboard the *Wasp* for a few minutes. Life did n't use to be dull for long. Thinks I, now I 'm off duty I 'll just tackle Josh for what he was so blasted set on telling me this morning. I 'd been thinking of what he 'd said, and how the doctor had miscalled me and I was n't quiet in my mind.

" Here 's Josh," says I to me, " calls me a damn thick-head, and here 's Surgeon calls me a damn fool; 't is six of one and half dozen of t' other," says I, " and here 's myself with half a sneaking guess that they 're right, though just why, Lord knows, I *don't*. But two of 'em anyway are men who 've seen the world more 'n I, and know a fool when they see him, maybe."

This part of the reasoning began to make me mad again. " Still," says I, " there 's no need of their jaw tackle running so free. One would suppose," says I to me, "that I'd been hurting Nancy's feelings a purpose, to hear Josh; and to hear Surgeon you'd believe I did n't know as well as he what a clipper she is. Now splice those two bits together, mate," thinks I, "and see what you get."

So I thought and calculated till it suddenly came to me that I'd maybe been rating Jim too heavy and myself too light, and just about then I concluded the next chance I got I'd square myself with Nancy and lay a new course. 'T was n't long before I got the chance. She'd not been on deck since the shindy with Pico, but she was up soon after we'd cut the prize out. At a handy minute I steps up.

" 'T was a pretty chase and a smart capture," says I, " Miss Nancy. It's a pity you should n't ha' seen it."

" The deck was n't the proper place for a woman," says she, " with such blackguards as your yellow Yankee is."

"Come," says I, "Miss, he's a Portugee; no Yankee would ever,"—I was going to say "insult you"—but she cut in—

"Never mind what he was, or what he said," and shut her mouth close together.

"Downs was there," says I, "and hit him a good one to teach him manners." She looked at me sort of cold and far-away.

"Yes," she says, "little as he is, he stood by like a man," says she.

"And yet," says I, not liking her to think the rest of us were not as keen to take up her fight as Downs, "he's the only one that heard——"

"Yes," says she, "some little men have quick ears."

Well, it was enough to rile a parson to hear the girl go on. You'd suppose that we all sat by and heard Pico abuse her and left it to poor little Jim to take it up. I wanted to tell her the rest of it, and if she'd been half way like any reasonable girl I ever knew she'd ha' seen how it all came about, but I knew she'd think I was blowing my own

horn, and talking what she once called
Yankee brag, so I said nothing about it. I
wanted to have a few words with her without a quarrel, howsomever, and so I said
how it did Jim very great credit, and how
his heart was in the right place; and several
other pleasant yarns I spun, thinking to
please her.

"Stow Jim," says she very sudden, and
looking up at me, "why don't you tell me
about yourself and the cut you got in the
ribs?" says she.

"Well, 't was but a scratch, anyhow, and
how did you know of it?"

"Surgeon told me," says she, then stopped
quick, as if she 'd said too much.

"How did he come to speak of it?" says I.

"None of your affair," she says, very airy,
"Surgeon and I are old friends," she adds
as if to explain.

"Well, no offence," I says; I was anxious
to keep on her good side, for she seemed for
the minute to be willing to treat me like a
white man.

"No, no offence, Bill, not a bit," says she, and laughed.

"What do you think of Surgeon?" says I, more to keep the talk running than anything else.

"Why, he's a very nice gentleman," says she, "and a good friend of yours, Bill."

"Is, hay?" says I, "he called me a damn fool to-day, if you call that friendly."

"What for?" says she, lifting her eyebrows and looking off to sea.

"Why," says I, then I got flustered, for I did n't know just how to get away from the question.

"Come, Bill, you must tell me;—tell me, Bill?"

"Well," says I, "he asked me if I 'd a sweetheart to home."

"Well," she says, still looking out to seaward and blushing just a little.

"And I says no." She looked at me then and her eyes seemed kind and friendly, I might almost say soft. "Well," she says slowly, in a low voice, "and what did he say?"

"Well," and now I wanted to back water but I could n't do it, and there was naught to do but go on. "Well," I says, " *he* says, ' there 's Nancy Barker.' "

I thought she 'd be in a rage at this, but she only said, " Well? "

" And I says, ' She 's well enough,' says I to him, ' but she 's Jim Downs's,' and he says, ' You 're a damn fool.' "

I looked at her then to see what she did. She was still looking out the hatch, not seeming to see anything, rather red and looking angry. " Well," I says, " that 's the yarn."

" That 's the yarn, is it," says she very slow.

" Yes," says I, " and I don't call that friendly, do you."

" Well," she says, " it 's always a friend's act, a true friend's act to speak the truth."

" What," says I, " you mean——"

" Bill," she says, quite cool and getting up from the step she 'd been sitting on, " if I ever knew a man who could rightly be

called that name, it 's you—yes, it is," she
cried suddenly flying into a rage and stamping her foot—"You 're a great silly baby
and a, a damn fool, and that 's what you
are," and down the hatch she flies leaving
me to wonder and get hot.

"It 's a nice coil this," says I to me—
"here 's three people say I 'm a damn fool
—one 's too old to lick, another 's my officer, and the third 's a girl, so I 've just got
to sit by and swallow it—and worse yet here
am I that 's beginning to think I am one my
blessed self and yet to save my life, Bill," says
I, " I can't read the signals." I went below
for a while, half worrying, half wanting to
swear. I was still below when I heard some
sound above, and then it came louder and I
knew we 'd sighted another sail. The crew
were gathered to the sides of the ship, some
of them in the main shrouds. Joe Martin,
the boatswain, was looking at the skyline
with his glass. " There 's three," at last he
said, " maybe more merchantmen, lads, maybe warships, for they 're looking for us,

Well, we 've got a bran-new sting ready,"
says he, laughing, " eh, boys."

"You 're right we have, boatswain, and
we want nothing better than to use it," says
gunner's mate.

Boatswain shook his head. " We 'll get
use enough for it," says he—"stinging 's
well enough, but not too many at once.
Still," says he, " I guess the ship can take
care of all she lays alongside of."

So we went for half an hour or more,
every one on the strain, for some way we felt
pretty sure we were in for more fighting, and
at about seven the chase, which was the most
weatherly of the four sail, began to signal
with lanterns.

" There 's a man-o'-war in the flock," says
boatswain then ; " even if the one we 're
chasing, is n't, for she 's signalling for aid."

The word was passed just then for boatswain, and he went aft. In a few minutes he
came back and spoke to several of the gun
captains. Then the word got among us that
we were bearing down upon a brig-o'-war

about the size of the *Reindeer*, and that 't was an even chance she 'd a mate at hand, so we 'd have to finish her up lively.

"This is the right shop to come to for quick work," says the boatswain, " now, lads, look alive when we beat to quarters."

All this time we were coming up to the chase, if you can call her that, seeing she was n't doing much running away. I had a little of the same feeling I 'd had when we were closing with the *Reindeer*, only this time 't was not so strong. I felt as sure as that my name was Bill Fry we 'd have her flag down inside an hour, "and yet should she put up as good a fight as the *Reindeer*," thinks I, "there will be a dozen good seamen less aboard the *Wasp* pretty soon."

This thought kind of kept hold of my mind as I walked up and down, now and again stopping to talk with the lads as they chatted in low tones about the fo'k'sle. I guess they all felt a bit as I did. They were confident of winning, even more, maybe, than before our first action, but they 'd seen

bloody death next hand to 'em, and they
did n't know when he'd get them by the
throat. Most of 'em were talking, clustered
forward, where they could see the brig we
were making for. Here and there one was
quiet and thoughtful, thinking maybe, of
wife or sweetheart to home, and one of
the quiet ones was I. I'd no wife or
sweetheart to home, but right here in
the *Wasp* was a lass I was loving, and loving very dear, in my way, which was stupid,
I guess, and slow. She'd called me a hard
name that very afternoon, and had gone
away leaving me to choke back and down
the feeling that once in a while would come
to me, that she really liked me a little.
Now, in a short time, the drum would call
us to quarters, and then who knew what was
to come.

Maybe she'd be sorry if they had to sew
me up and slide me off a plank in the morning. But I'd never said anything to her that
would make her take any special interest in
me. I was a fool to her, as a fool she'd feel

sorry for me, and there was an end. I could n't bear to go into action and that word the last between us. The night was coming on, and we were gaining fast on the brig; we'd be called to quarters soon. "There's one thing," I says to me, "she always *is* bound to think a wise man's act, and that is to be fond of her, and I'm going to let her know that in that quarter my head's as good as the next man's." I thought I'd go below and hang about the waist of the ship a minute, on chance of seeing her.

I went to the hatchway, and there she stood. There she stood, no cap on, her hair tumbled over her shoulders, a white kerchief about her throat, and a quiet, strained look to her face. Because of the dark, she hardly knew me as I came up, then, when she did, she looked at me in a way as if I'd come right along the same wind with her thoughts.

"Miss Nancy," says I, looking down at her, "here's the fool back," says I, not knowing just what to say.

She did n't speak, but rested her hands on the rail of the companion-way, and looked at me with her lips a little apart, and breathing rather quick.

"He wants to know," I went on, "Bill Fry, the fool, Miss, seeing he's going into action, if you won't wish him not Plymouth Jail, maybe, but luck, this time," and I put out my hand, and as I did the roll of the drum rang out clear and loud. I gave one look at her, for she was quiet, and turned to go, when she caught me by the arm and pulled me—she was a strong lass—almost down the hatch.

"Wait," says she, "I am first, give me your hand!" She took it and pressed it hard, and I found she'd put a little smooth coin into it. "That's for luck," she said, and sprang down the hatchway. 'T was the sixpence with the hole in it she'd given me two months before and I'd given back.

She stopped at the foot of the companion-way and watched me dumfounded standing there. "'T is for good luck, good luck, Will," she called; "'t is a lucky six-pence."

I never heeded the men running here and there, the bustle and the roar; I never heeded my gun captain's cursing me and yelling to me to look alive ; I jumped down the stair and caught her hand. "Miss," I said, all in a tremble.

"Oh, not Miss, Nancy—Nancy, Nancy, stupid," she cried, and threw her arms about my neck and kissed me, then sprang away and was gone. I stood like one dazed. Happy was I? That 's not the word, drunk, I guess, is nearer.

God knows how long I 'd 'a' stood there, if a hand had n't gripped my shoulder and the gun captain's voice yelled into my ear : "Bill, you lubber, are you skulking or crazy? Come up here!" I turned and shook him off.

"Hands off, mate," says I, "I 'm coming. Skulking aint in my family, but crazy I may be," says I, as I followed on deck, "but God help me, I hope not." Into my mouth for safe keep I slips the sixpence, and in a second more was at my gun.

'T was dark enough by now, but the brig's battle lanterns were lit, and so were ours, o' course, and the two crafts were marks enough for those as handled guns. The brig was still signalling, for help maybe, the Lord knows she needed it, but Captain Blakely had picked her out and was going to get her, consort or no. Suddenly she lets go a gun. It made a noise, but where the shot went we did n't know, not into us surely. Then she lets go another! 'T was good for a salute and that was all. The *Wasp* came right along and as still as the *Flying Dutchman*, no cheering, no guns.

So it went for nearly three quarters of an hour I should guess. 'T was not so hard to stand as in the *Reindeer* fight, for we felt these lubbers could n't shoot, should they fire on us again before we were ready to open, which they did n't. Manners's lads were gunners in act, as well as name. About 9.30 I saw the crew of the bloody little shifting carronade we'd taken out of the *Rein-deer*, a useful gun it was, as well we knew, begin to jump about, and in a minute off she goes, and 't was easy guessing, by the rattle of truck upon the brig's deck, she'd taken her word straight.   Three or four guns replied, all without carrying much meaning in their answer, so to speak, and then Blakely, like the game cock he was, fearing just one thing, that she might get away, puts up helm and runs to leeward of her, and ranged right alongside, and let go a broadside into her quarter.

For a few minutes 't was as hot as the *Reindeer* action, maybe hotter.   So close we were that a man was knocked off his feet by a gun wad.   We did n't know then who the craft was we were fighting; she was a big one, and her tops seemed black with men. She fired high, as the British most always did, and the ropes and rigging caught it pretty hot.   She got only four shots into our hull.   I heard 'em crash and tear, and I heard a cry from below.

"My God!" I thinks, "Nancy 's below there," and it shows how I felt towards the lass when I say I left the gun and was going in a kind of wild way to the hatchway.

Some one caught me by the arm and swung me round. "You trying to skulk, Fry?" says he. 'T was the ship's doctor.

This brought me to myself.

"I was afraid she 'd been struck."

"Struck, you rascal, she 'll never strike!" he roared.

"Not the ship, sir," I said.

"What then?"

"Why, Nancy."

"Oh, Nancy! You get back to your gun. She 's aft in the ward-room safe enough; get back to your gun," and back I went.

But there was only a few minutes more of this, for the brig had got nigh punishment enough. Her officers maybe were gallant men, indeed they must ha' been to do as well as they had, but they were not of the William Manners kind. He 'd have let us get under his lee and glad of it; or he 'd ha'

sailed his craft right onto our deck, if so be
he could. But this brig was done dinner
without the extra ration of boarding.

We 'd been at it from our first gun to the
time she lay still, about half an hour maybe.
Then one of the officers hailed her and asked
had she struck? A musket shot and one
gun replied. She had some life left, and we
gave her a couple more broadsides, then quit
for a minute as she did n't answer, and 't is
no credit to pound a whipped man. This
time when we hailed we got an answer.

She had struck, and we began to lower
away a boat. Just as we were doing so
comes a cry of another craft close under our
stern, coming up in the dark.

Sure enough, and a war vessel, too—a brig
like the one we 'd just silenced. There was
quick work for a few minutes aboard the
Wasp, you may lay to that.

To run away? Not at all.

'T was the Captain's wish to engage the
second brig as he 'd done the first.

She came across our stern while we were
still putting things tidy, to give her a polite

reception, and let us have a broadside that cut us up a bit aloft, then stood for the brig we 'd just whipped, which was burning lights and firing guns of distress. We were going to engage the fresh one, but two more sails were made out just then, and it was thought best to go on our course, which we did.

I have heard since that the brig we fought, sunk soon after—that she was the *Avon*, 18, and the brig that came up was the *Castilian*, 18, and following her, *H. M. S. Tartarus*. So we were wise to slip away, though 't was generally believed among the men that we could ha' whipped the *Castilian* had she been alone, for we were nigh as good as new, and only three men short. Two dead, poor Joe Martin, the boatswain, as true a soul and good a boatswain as ever whistled a man aloft, and Henry Staples, the quarter gunner. Two men were wounded; one of them was Josh Sewall. He was old, too old to rally, and the day after the fight, though he was not hard hit, he was very bad, and the Surgeon looked grave.

.   .   .   .   .   .

The morning after the fight I was busy
just abaft the foremast when I looked up
and found Nancy standing by me.   I got up,
there was no one in sight at the minute, we
were well hidden, and put my arm about her
and kissed her.

. She did n't mind it; she seemed to be
pleased with me; and we said a few words
to each other, no matter what, 't is no use
writing 'em down.   I 'll never want 'em again
to say to any living woman, and they were
too private for even this log.   I guess we
had finally understood each other.

"So, Will," she says, sitting down by me
on the deck, "you were going to desert your
gun last night, were you?"

"There 's just one person in all the world
could make me do that," I says, bragging a
little, I suppose, but you know I was talking
to my sweetheart, "and that 's you, Nancy;
but how did you know it?"

"The Surgeon," says she, looking very sly,
and reaching a hand under cover of the sail
I was mending.

I took it, though I can't tell why I put that down here, only perhaps, because up to now I 'd been so blind, and a day or two before would ha' supposed she 'd put her hand under the canvas to keep it warm.

"Now, Nancy," says I, holding her hand very tight, "we aint said much, you nor I, but we understand each other, don't we, lass?"

"I 'm sure I can't speak for you," says she. "No, no, Will," says she, "not here, not again—not now, anyhow, for there 's Mr. Downs standing by the mizzen-shrouds."

"Blast Mr. Downs," says I; "I suppose he has——"

"Oh, Will," she says, very quiet and serious, "he never did, and you must n't talk that way to me," says she.

"Well, I beg pardon," says I; "but, Nancy, that young beggar Joe said *he* had—often—in Plymouth.'

"Perhaps," says she, quite cool, then, hot, "and I boxed his blooming ears well for him—the young neddy," says she, and then,

looking at me in a way that made everything
snug again, " I did n't know *you* then,
Will."

Just then boatswain's mate came along by
and I went on stitching canvas, for you can't
stitch with one hand.   But boatswain's
mates are n't passing all the time, and by
and by we were talking as before.

" Nancy," says I, "you know I used to
think Josh knew more 'n he told me, about
the vivandeer business."

"Well," says she, "you see, I 'm beginning
to talk like a Yankee—I guess, you see, Will,
I 'm beginning to 'guess' already ; he did.
Why, you 're the greatest stupid I ever
knew," says she, laughing at some memory,
maybe, that came to her.

" I 'll tell you now how it all was," she
goes on, holding my hand very close and
leaning my way.   " Tell me one thing first
that you 've forgot," she says, quite sudden.

I began to think.

" Oh, oh, oh," says she, as if very provoked
and yet laughing, too, " do you call yourself

an able seaman, yet here am I have to lay
the course for you all the while? Why, you
have n't said, ' I love you, Nancy.' "

I looked at her, but she would n't meet my
eyes.

" Lass," says I, quite low, " I did n't think
that was needed."

" Yes it is," she cries, " it is, and anyhow
I want you to—say you love me, say it
quick."

I let go her hand, for I needed my arm.
" My dear," says I, " I love you better than
I can tell you, far better than I love myself,
and I 'm pretty fond of Bill Fry, too."

" And so am I," says she, and put her face
up towards mine.

This log is n't needed to call back to my
mind that evening. 'T is clear yet in my
memory. The good *Wasp* heeling a bit as
she stood along on a brisk breeze over her
port beam—twilight coming on, and a star in
the westward, for we were pointed towards
home. A sailor was singing soft, the other
side the hatchway, some hymn tune 't was,

that I had heard before. And many 's the time since then I 've sat in meeting and heard that tune. And as I lean back in my old seat by the wall, I hear no more preaching, see nothing of the folk around me, but the noise I 'll hear will be the hum of a steady breeze aloft, the creak of the tackle, and the wash of the sea, till I almost believe that I 'll find beside me, when I open my eyes, my dear, dear lass, and love, Nancy Barker.

CHAPTER VII.

HOW THE WARD-ROOM DRANK TO NANCY BARKER.

I 'VE no wish to speak here of the prizes we took, for we overhauled three or four between the 1st and the 21st of the month. We burned or scuttled all of them and took the crews aboard. 'T was odd enough that Nancy would have no more to do with her countryman, but since she 'd made up her mind to be American by annexation, she 'd no wish to look back.

All these days we 'd see each other every day a little while, sometimes by ourselves, sometimes with others about. There was difference enough between such meetings to make me look ahead with a bit of impatience to the end o' the cruise. We were very careful about Jim Downs, for I knew he was sparking Nancy, or had been, and would be the wrong man to know our secret; that was *my* reason, Nancy's was to keep him trotting for her just so long as she could.   And that 's the truth, by thunder.

" Tell the poor swab," says I to her.

" And make him unhappy for the rest of the cruise? " says she.

" Gammon, lass," I says—" it 's not that, my dear," I says, " but you want the beggar's polite little tricks when I 'm on duty," says I, " and maybe if anything happens to me——"

" Come, Will," says she, " that 's an old joke by now, you know."

" Well," says I, " and that 's true, but 't is one of the few jokes I know;—never mind, Jim," says I, remembering the trick he played me once and how he 'd acted off and on with me, aboard ship, " maybe 't will be the kindest way and——"

" Do you know what he asked me to do at L'Orient? " says she, suddenly.

" Not a bit," says I.

" Well, to run off to England with him—

he said he 'd desert and get aboard an English packet that came in while we lay there."
Nancy always spoke of us as *we*, by now.

"The sneak," says I—" and you would n't go away with a deserter—hay?"

"Not that one," she says, smiling.

"Nor me either, I hope, if I were one as well," says I.

"No," says she, quite slow, "no, Bill, I don't think that I would," says she. This by good luck was one of the times we were by ourselves.

So everything went along pretty pleasant. I guess Surgeon saw how things were, for he told me one day that I had more intelligence than he gave me credit for, and one day again he says:

"Bill, I suppose you 'll not be following the sea after this cruise." He sort of cocked his eye at me, and I knew what he was driving at.

"Well, sir," says I, "I 've heard as how Captain Blakely left a wife ashore to go this cruise, and maybe I 'll be able to do as well as he on the next—give me a little time ashore."

"I'll give you ten days," says he, "before that clipper girl, that privateer," says he, calling her the same name he'd used before, "takes charge of the ship and turns you adrift in the dingy," and he laughed hearty.

The 21st day of September we took a brig, the *Atalanta*. She was armed with eight guns, and was a prize worth the saving. We threw a prize crew into her with Mr. Geisinger, a midshipman, in command, and sent her home. Captain Blakely had me into his cabin before we parted company with the brig.

"Bill," he says, as if it came natural to him, and I found out later that they talked a good bit of Nancy and me in the ward-room, so 't was as if he knew me better, maybe, than he did some of the others of the crew.

"Bill," says the Captain, "the *Atalanta*'s going straight for a home port, and it's my intention to send Miss Nancy along of her;

this ship 's no place for her, though 't is as
safe as a church so far as my lads go."

"You can tie to it, 't is so, sir," says I,
saluting, "and please your honor," I says,
"if I may speak, is it not a better place than
the *Atalanta* brig?"

"Why, Bill," he says, "can't you trust
her?" and laughed a bit.

This stirred me up. "Trust her, sir," says
I, "trust her I can wherever her own mind
stands at the wheel, your honor," says I;
"but who 's to say some bloody British
privateersman may not snap the brig up?
Aboard the *Wasp*, sir, she 's safe—naught
short of a 74 can get her out of us, and we
can show heels to the best line-o'-battle ship
in King George's Navy, sir," I says.

I 'm no fool, in some ways at any rate,
and I knew what I said would please Captain Blakely, and please him it did.

"Well, Doctor," says he, smiling, to Dr.
Clarke, who was with him, "Bill 's a great
sea lawyer, aint he; there 's something in
what he says, too. But Bill," he went on,

she 'd be safe in a British crew, for she 's an
English girl, you know."

"Beg your pardon, Captain," I says, "but
she 's as good a Yankee by now as Bill
Fry."

"Well, well," says Blakely after a minute's thought, "I'll put you aboard the
Atalanta in the prize crew, my man, and
you can look after Miss," says he; "you 're
a good hand to lose though," says he, talking half to himself, "too good almost, eh,
Doctor?"

The Doctor kind o' shook his head. He
wanted to help me and Nancy home safe,
and yet he did n't like to advise against anything the Captain might suggest. As for me,
it 's the truth I was for the time so pleased
to think of getting my girl to shore and going along of her, that I guess I could n't
help showing it. I waited for the Captain,
and by and by he says again :

"Well, Bill, I 'll send you aboard the
Atalanta, and you can look out for the lass
yourself."

I saluted and went forward, and in a jiffy
found Nancy at the door of her cabin and
told her.   At first she seemed as happy as I
was, till I happened to say that Captain
said I was most too good a man to lose.
This I said to brag a bit, and I got caught
up for it.   She was quite sober for a minute,
and then she says:

"Will," says she, "if I must leave you, then
I must—I'm not afraid, with our men aboard
the brig," she meant the lads from the
Wasp, ."and I'll find a safe place to wait
for you in America—you can send me a
letter to your mother, you know," says she;
"but, Will, I can't have you, that I love so,
and respect as much, leave duty when you're
needed, to look out for me."   She just put
her arms about my neck and looked me
right in the face.

"But, lass,——" says I.

"No, dear," she says, breaking in, "you
must not go."   Then she put her head on
my shoulder and cried.

I thought she'd changed her mind, and

2

says I : " Nancy, it 's all right ; there 'll be no more work, and it 's best I should——"·

" Oh, Will," she says, stopping her sobs, " I want you so, I want you so, but dear, don't you see how proud it makes me to think they don't like to spare my lad from his gun. Maybe they won't send me, but if they do, it 's go alone. 'T will be but a few months, dear."

Well, the upshot of this was that that afternoon I stood before the Captain again. There were several officers with him, and the Surgeon too.

" Well, says he, pleasant, for he was always that way with his men, " what now, Bill— is n't the young lady willing to leave us with you ? "

" Your honor," says I, " she 's ready to go if so be she must, but I 'll not go along of her. If there 's need of me aboard, as asking your pardon, I thought from what you said this morning there might be, why I shipped for work aboard the *Wasp*, sir, and on the *Wasp* I 'll serve, unless your honor drives me off," says I, quite red by now.

The Captain looked at me very steady. "You mean this, my lad," said he very gentle, but in a voice that made me happy to have said my say as I said it. Then he looked round at the others. "That 's the sort of seamen I *cannot* afford to put aboard a prize, gentlemen," says he, and they all said something, never mind what, about my being the true sort.

I was feeling pretty proud, when a sudden idea came into my head. 'T was Nancy to praise for this, not me. And I spoke up quick:

"Your honor," says I, "I should tell you and the gentlemen here one thing, for I calculate to be honest," says I, "I would have gone to-day in the *Atalanta*, and happy to at that," says I, "but, sir, my lass, 't is she won't have it, for, 'Will,' says she, 'I 'm that proud to think they value you, that want you as I do, I 'll go alone sooner than take you away from duty,' says she, and so, Captain and gentlemen," says I, "it stands this way."

Well, before the Captain could speak the Surgeon hit the table with his fist.

" By the Lord," says he, " Captain Blakely,
you can't put that lass in a prize crew
neither," says he, " let her stay aboard, let
her stay if she 'll take the chances."

The Captain looked to the other officers.
" What do *you* say, gentlemen ? "

" Why, if she 's willing, let her stay," says
one, and the other, who seemed to be a jolly
lad in a way, says : " By all means, Captain,
she 'll heart the crew up ; and I suggest if it
suit you, sir, we drink her health."

" With all my heart," says the Captain,
and raps on the table. I was going to go
but he stops me.

" Wait, my man," says he, " you of all
men should drink that health." When the
boy brought in the glasses and a bottle of
sherry and we 'd all filled, the Captain nods
to the Surgeon and says he, " Clarke, give us
a sentiment," and Surgeon says, " I give
you the last Yankee invention," says he,
" a man-o'-war's-woman—here 's Nancy Barker !" says he, and we took it down at
a toss.

"Now, Bill," says the Captain, "you can go and tell the young lady she takes the chances of war." And so I saluted and went forward.

In this way things ran along for more than two weeks. Each day I'd see something of Nancy; sometimes only a word did we have, sometimes maybe a half hour or more. One day I remember she came back to the talk we had before about my folks.

"Will," says she,—for some days when she'd feel special kind she always called me that, though 't was Bill when in a hurry, maybe, or perhaps vexed with me,—"do you think your mother's going to like me?" she asks, quite soft, as if afraid what I might say.

"She'll like anything I do, I guess," says I; "anyhow I'm not obliged to lie at the same dock," says I.

"Still," says she, "I'd like her to like me."

"Well I don't know how she can help it— that's the fact," says I.

"But, Will," says she, "I'm afraid for my language—it's too, too sailor-like, Will, for you know it's what I've mostly heard all my life. You won't be telling her now that I called you a damn fool, will you, dear?"

"God bless you, my lass," says I with a roar, for I had to laugh to hear her so simple, yet kind of anxious, too; "she's called me the same many's the time—not in those words maybe, but meaning the same; and you did but tell the truth when all's said and done."

"Will, are you sure there's no sweetheart waiting for you in Portsmouth, lad?"

"Sure am I," says I, "and I wish I was so sure of a long life."

"And has there never been one, dear?"

I didn't answer at once and she ran on, not waiting: "I'm glad there hasn't, for indeed 't is plain there's never been one— you don't act like a man that's kept company somehow."

"How's that?" says I, willing to leave

Lindy and the way she treated me out of
the talk.

"Why," she says, laughing in my face,
"I 'm just guessing, that 's all, like a Yankee
that I 'm going to be."

"Oh," says I, "'t is well for you it 's broad
day and the deck full of sailors, or I 'd take
my pay, so much for a guess, like a church
fair," I says, and she runs away below.

So things went along. I had but little to
say or do with Jim Downs all this time, but
I 'd seen him with Nancy quite frequent. I
never worried much about it, but sometimes
the swab made me angry by his stupid ways.
He might ha' seen how matters stood with
half an eye. 'T was an open secret abaft the
mizzen-mast I reckon, and some of my
mates were poking fun at me much of the
time.

Now old Josh Sewall, as I said, had been
wounded in the fight with the *Avon* and
had n't picked up. 'T was nice to see the
way the girl looked after him. If he 'd been
her father she could n't ha' been gentler

with him.   The old man always had a liking
for her and she 'd read to him and fetch him
this and that, from the galley, the cook would
fix up for him, for he was as well liked an old
lad as you could find.

One day in the early part of October he
was very bad, out of his head a good half
the time and calling to people we never
knew or heard of.   He was the first I 'd
ever heard a-raving and 't was hard to listen
to.   Nancy stayed close by him most of the
time.   Lord, how the poor old lad would
shout.   Nancy crept up to the deck for a
bit of fresh air, and I found her there.

"O Will," says she, "he 's talking of
some one named Sarah," says she, "and it 's
cruel hard to hear him, and see him pipe
his poor old eyes and throw his arms
around."

"There now, lass," says I, for she began
to cry, "you 're piping your own pretty eyes
and 't will do no good.   It's likely his mother
he 's talking of."

"His mother!" says she, "do you call

your mothers by their first names in America?
—no, you stupid, 't is his wife."

"Or daughter," says I.

"No, wife, I tell you," says Nancy very
set, "and O Will, do you think when you
get to be as old as Josh you 'll remember
me? Come below a minute and see the
poor old man."

Down we went and up to Josh's bunk
in the steerage. He was talking fast and
high, and I heard names that used to be
heard when the navy was just out the shell
—Jones and Biddle and Preble and Somers.
Josh had been following the sea since the
first war, the war of Independence. Then
of a sudden all this stopped and he said very
distinct:

"Sarah, here 's your man Josh," and then
again and again.

I had to go on deck, and glad of the
chance, for my scuppers were running.

CHAPTER VIII.

HOW JIM DOWNS TOOK FRENCH LEAVE.

WE had sighted a sail early on this day and by now had got close to her and hove her to. We found her to be the Norwegian packet *Adonis*, and we sent a boat off to her. With the boat went Jim Downs with some private letters of several officers aboard to parties in Europe.

The poor beggar had been very down in his mouth for a fortnight and was that pale and sick-looking that many who did n't like him pitied him. His action with the Portugee brigantine *Pico*, as Josh used to describe the little scuffle he and the yellow beggar had on the fo'k'sle, had made him more friends than he 'd had up to then. He was sick for news o' land and needed change of some kind, I reckon, so he was let go aboard

the *Adonis* as a kind of treat, for by and long
a treat it is, when you 've been six weeks or
more at sea, to look at new faces, and hear
fresh news, other than the sulky mugs and
surly lies you run athwart on your prizes.
Well, the boat was gone a long time—then
back it comes—we saw some kind of excitement aft as the officer in charge reported.
Then off goes the boat again and we saw the
officer board the *Adonis* once more. By and
by we could tell there was something up
aboard the packet for there was handshaking going on and then down the lad-
der to the cutter comes our officer and two
strangers.

When the boat got near the *Wasp*, we 'd
lined the bulwarks to see what was up, and
presently we saw the Captain off his hat and
cry out some hail, then the other officers,
and then who cheers but Bill Fry, for sitting
cosy and cool in the stern of the boat were
Lieutenant McKnight and Master Lyman of
my old ship the *Essex*. They had been exchanged, as it turned out, and were bound

to England from Rio Janeiro, as the readiest way home, when they met us.

Well, the lads cheered and cheered as the word ran forward, and pretty soon we could see the handshaking on the quarter-deck. I kind of edged up near to where the Captain and the two *Essex* men stood. By and by McKnight caught sight of me. He thought he knew me, then he thought he did n't. But presently he walks up to me—

"Where have you served, my man?" says he.

"On the *Essex*, sir," says I, saluting.

"I knew it," he says, "you must have been sent off in one of the prize crews."

"The *Hector's*, sir."

"Well, well," says he, "you missed bloody glory and the stiffest business I ever heard of, by being aboard her," says he.

"Well, sir," says I, "we've had some pretty hot duff to swallow aboard the *Wasp*, sir," I says.

"Yes, yes," he says, "I know your captain and I'll go bail for him to keep you busy." Here the Captain takes him by the arm.

"Come, McKnight," says he, "come below and let us get a word of Porter. I'll spin my yarn, and get yours. We've had no news of the *Essex* for the last eight months." The Captain and all but the officer of the deck went below. There was more going and coming between the two ships; both McKnight and Lyman went back to the *Adonis* for a short spell and another trip the boat made after that, but finally we parted company and she was soon hull down. It did n't take long for the story of the staunch old *Essex* to get over the ship, and for several hours 't was all the men talked or thought about. 'T is history now, well known, I guess, how the game little frigate lay in Valparaiso harbor ready to fight, yes, daring 'em on, either British ship that pleased, and one of them, the *Phœbe*, bigger than her. But they did n't please. They 'd come out to get Captain Porter and his ship, and 't was a risk they could n't

afford, to talk single with him an hour, or
maybe two.

Every tar that's fought under the gridiron knows how Porter might ha' raked the
Phœbe when she fouled him running into
harbor, and how because the British Commodore swore that he meant no offence the
Yankee Captain let it pass. And every
man-jack has heard how the Britisher sent
neutrality to hell and pitched onto the little
Essex, crippled by her topmast going off in
a gale, and pounded her from a distance, till
she lay a blazing wreck with her cockpits
full of dead and the dead and wounded lit-
tering the ship from stem to stern.

Pounded her from a distance, mind ye—no
coming aboard, not they; had they tried it
—but well, well! I get now so hot over it,
though 't was years ago, I can but rip and
curse. 'T was my old ship, the ship I first
learned the man-o'-war's-man's trade in, and
I own I felt like a baby when I heard how
she 'd been taken.

But Lord, she took toll, too! And had

she been able to get in closer quarters the
story maybe would have been another one.

Well it must ha' done the two officers we
took aboard good to hear what we'd been
doing, and the spirit of them showed out in
their coming on deck dressed again in the
States uniform, volunteer officers for the rest
of the cruise. The men all gathered aft and
cheered them hearty, and McKnight taking
off his hat says:

"Lads, we 've shipped aboard the *Wasp*
along with Captain Blakely, because we like
him, because we belong under the old bunting yonder, and because, by the Lord," says
he, suddenly, " we 've a score to pay John
Bull, and we 're honest men that pay our
debts."

Well, such talk was the talk for the *Wasp's*
crew. I know I 've said it here before, but
it keeps coming up to me, and that is the
spirit that ran through the entire ship's company. They did n't seem to care about going home—they were more anxious to cruise
and fight, almost, than the officers them-

selves, if such a thing could be. They got it straight from one man, and that was Blakely. With his gentle face and pleasant manners, he was the deadest set man for fighting I ever saw. And 't is truth that the presence of the two officers from the *Essex* seemed to heat things up. I heard it said that Blakely had sent a challenge by the *Adonis* to any two British brigs to fight him.* It was like him, if it wa' n't true; and you may call it brag, but from what I saw the night we sunk the *Avon*, we could ha' given an account of 'em.

Now, while everything was full of stir and as much in a wax as things can ever be on board a man-o'-war, owing to the officers from the *Essex* and their news, no one came to notice that Jim Downs was n't aboard. By and by purser's clerk did, and then there was a hot search. But 't was no use.

The swab was gone.

He 'd hid himself aboard the *Adonis* and got away. The Norwegian was out o' sight

* Niles's *Register.*

when we knew she had him aboard, and 't was hardly worth while to chase her.

"Let the little skunk go," says the gunner's mate to me, "he's the fly in the ointment that causeth it to stink."

Gunner's mate was one of the most pious talking, aye and thinking too, aboard the ship, but in action he had a gift in the way of talk that he did n't learn at meeting, by thunder!

Well, I guess 't was generally considered a good riddance aboard the *Wasp*. I wanted to tell Nancy, for I 'd not seen her since morning, and so I went to her cabin. The door was closed. I rapped.

"Who is it?" says she.

"'T is I, Bill," I answered, and I heard her jump to the door and then she threw it open. God help me, I never saw her look so wild and strange!

"What," says she, hardly able to talk, "do you come here, you liar, you liar! I know you for what you are, Mr. Bill Fry," she cries, stamping her foot and throwing

13

her hand with a bit of a letter in it, almost against my face, " Oh, you 've no sweetheart at home, you never had one—oh no, no," she says, for I was too hit all of a sudden to say a word ; " I 've word of it, mate,—I know the bloody lies that you 've been spinning out to me now."

She was getting back into her old fo'k'sle way of talk.

" Lass," says I, " for God's sake, what 's come to you," for I thought she 'd gone crazy.

" What 's come to me ?" says she, with a laugh that I could n't bear to hear, " this is what 's come to me," and she held the letter towards me.   I saw 't was Jim Downs's fist on it.

" Well," I says, trying to be cool, though temper was getting to weather of me, " that 's from the poor sneak that 's just stowed away on the *Adonis* and deserted. T is likely a lot of blasted lies, but read 'em lass, if you won't let me do so," for she snatched it back when I tried to take it.

" No need o' that," she says, "no need to tell *you* of Lindy ; ah, you know it's true, you know it is."

"But," says I, "I never lied to you of her; I gave her up when I left, when I left, Nancy, I knew she did n't care for me, and so help me God I never did really care for her. Josh Sewall will tell you, I left her, and glad to be away, lass, 't is the truth."

" Oh, don't tell me more lies, you mean sea lawyer," says she, shaking her head. "Josh Sewall dying, too—a good witness for one that does n't want the truth told. What about the token you sent her by Caleb Whaley, eh, what about the gold anchor with the wreath about it ? "

"Lass," says I, trying hard to talk cool, "'t is true I sent such a knicknack to the girl, and with it went good-by, and no word of promise, and she cared less about me and what I was doing than she cared for the trinket, which Caleb says was little enough."

" Oh, stow your talk," says the girl, " I 'll ask no more questions, my man,—you need tell no more lies ; why don't you," says she, asking a question right off, " tell me to ask Caleb Whaley, who 's dead this six weeks? Dead men tell no tales, Mr. ·Bill," she says, "but live ones make up for 'em," and then she laughed again in a way that cut my heart.

" Nancy," says I, trying once more to get sense into her head, " listen, for God's sake, lass——— "

" Don't you dare speak to me that way," she said, very fierce, and I never knew any one so hot all through with temper. " I never want you nor any other Yankee to speak to me again. God forgive me," she says, crying, but only out of rage, " for forgetting old Plymouth and my birthright as an English girl. I 'll be put aboard the first ship we—you, I mean—you, you Yankees heave to, and go anywhere—anywhere away from Yankees and—and lies." And here she broke out into a sort of cry, pushed me from the door and shut and locked it.

I went on deck and was sent aloft almost

as soon as I got there. Lying out on the
yards furling sail I had n't the chance to do
much thinking of what had just took place.
When you 're aloft your brains must be in
your fingers. If you let 'm run around trying to explain why a lass lets a broadside
into you without hailing you, as it were,
you 're apt to take a long drop, and I was
always the man to look after my own skin.

Yet it won't do to say I wa' n't cut up, and
worse.   If it had been plain anger bothering
me I 'd ha' weathered it handily, but the girl
was so much to me that to think of her going so wrong about me, was by itself enough
to cut me to the heart. And to think she
had called me a liar, and believed it, and one
witness dying, and one dead, and the whelp
that made all the trouble safe away where I
could n't get my hands on his windpipe!
Well, when I got to deck again and let these
things come over me, I was in what they
call a state of mind ! I knew 't was the wise
thing to let the girl cool off, and so I waited.

CHAPTER IX.

HOW JOSH SEWALL WENT TO SARAH.

I DID n't see Nancy again that night nor the following day. So the next night I got to see the Surgeon a minute. I told him the whole yarn and he believed me.

"I 'll see her to-morrow, Bill," he says— "She 's a girl of sense, and I 'll make it all ship-shape again," says he.

To-morrow was a long time a-coming, and when about eight bells Surgeon comes alongside and takes me to the rail by the mizzen-shrouds, it seemed as if I 'd waited a week.

" Bill," he says, " let the girl alone. She 's in a curious frame of mind," says he; those were his words—" and the least said to her for a while the better. She thinks we 're all liars and calls us Yankees, which last, praise God," says he laughing, " I 'm glad to say

is true.   But just at the present she 's a
fitter subject for the Chaplain than for me.   I
think she 's got as lively a command of lingo
of a sea-faring kind," says he, " as any old
salt that follows the sea.   At present she 's
down on everything, her luck to begin with,
and the whole ship's company from Captain
Blakely to William Fry, and him especially,"
says he laughing.   " So Bill, let her cool a
day or two more.   As it is, I 'm afraid she 'll
fire the ship yet."

I thanked him and allowed it would be
best to go by his steering.   It made me
smile, sick as I felt, to think of the girl laying the Surgeon aboard, and I knew 't would
ha' been the same with the Chaplain.

That evening I heard word that Josh
Sewall was going.   I went to the old lad's
side in the steerage.   Half a dozen of the
men were standing around, and kneeling by
his bed was Nancy Barker.   She never
looked at us but watched the poor old man's
face and now and then took his hand when it
was quiet.

For two days he 'd talked and mumbled all
the time, always coming back to the same
old word—" Sarah, here 's your man Josh,"
and as we stood about him he struck up
again.

I 'd known him fifteen years, off and on,
and never heard he was married or ever had
been. But Jack's marriage-certificate is his
word, I guess, and there 's many has a wife
in every port, as they say, but Josh was not
that build; and if so be there was, or had
been, a Sarah with a claim to the old man,
I 'm willing to believe Josh was her man,
aye, her man and no other's.

As he moaned and called out, Nancy
would kind of soothe him, now and again
sobbing to herself, and Josh would sometimes hold her hand in both of his, and then
he 'd lie quiet. Sick and crazy as the poor
old lad was, he could tell the hands that held
him belonged to a woman who was caring
for him and was sorry for him.

The Surgeon in a few minutes told us we
must leave him to himself. The girl might

stay if she would, he said. I could n't help stepping close to her a minute.

"Nancy," I says, very low, "I swear to you here by old Josh's death-bed that——"

"Hush," says she, very cold, "this is n't the place for, for what is n't true."

"But it is, it is, lass—I care no more for that girl than——"

"Then you 're false to her and that 's nigh as bad," says she. "No, Mr. Fry," she says, very quiet, "let 's have no more words about the thing." And just then the Surgeon ordered me away.

We buried Josh that evening, as we 'd buried near two-score good seamen, our own and British, since the cruise began. A good loyal man, handy with his cutlass, an all round, first-class, able-bodied seaman, was buried with old Josh Sewall.

'T was a calm evening, though it looked like weather to the sou'east, and the splash of the body as it slipped off the plank sent ripples out and around like a stone in a mill-pond.

Josh could and would swear, many 's the
time; and I 've seen him obliged to make a
dozen tacks in a straight-laid course, because
he 'd a little too much Medford between
decks, but not often.   This was all top-
hamper.   The hull of the man was sound as
oak, and there 's a snug berth for Josh aloft,
if there is for any one.   No one of us knew
where he was born, what corner of the States
he hailed from, but he went to his long
home and to Sarah, as he wanted to go, by
way of the sea.

We had hardly finished with the burial
service when the man on the lookout forward
sighted a sail on the port bow.   'T was a
pleasant change and like the life on sea.
There 's too much on hand, what with the
weather to watch, the ship to look to, and
the skyline to search for sail, to spend much
time thinking of a dead messmate, however
good he may ha' been, and we were all on
the jump, to rights.   I guess the liking for
prizes is like the taste for rum.   The more
you get the more you want, and some time

had passed since we 'd lit up the night with a bonfire. But before dusk had settled we knew 't was no merchantman we 'd sighted; no, nor no brig-o'-war this time.

" 'T is a corvette or a frigate," says one of my mates whose eyes were keener than mine, " and it 's dollars to shillings," says he, " it 's a frigate, for I never saw a corvette of her size."

Sure enough, word soon blew about the fo'k'sle that we 'd sighted a frigate, a 44 maybe, certainly not under a 36, and what 's more, we were not going to run.

" Run !" says an old lad nigh me, " run after her, maybe," and that 's how the lads all felt.

By and by I heard that John Rowe had been aft on some duty, and he 'd heard what the Captain said about her as he sized her up from the quarter deck. Says John:

" Captain Blakely says," says he, " ' She 's a big one, Tillinghast,' he says, and Tillinghast says, ' She 's no more to fight than two brigs at once, is she?' and the Captain laughs kind of quiet and says, 'That's what we're going to find out,' and then all the officers laughed, and looked at each other as if to say, 'That's what we were thinking.' Then up comes Mr. McKnight from below and takes a look, then says he, 'You're not sheering off are you, Blakely?' and then, getting the ship's course, says he, 'Why, she's not so big after all.' 'Wait,' says Captain, and just then the boatswain's whistle pipes up, the ship tacked, and down we went along the wind head on to the frigate. McKnight turned sudden and gripped Blakely's hand, and says he, 'Captain Blakely, you're a man, there's a score to settle,' says he, and Captain says, 'The time's come, then.'"

So we men knew that fight was the word, and we knew what's more, that we'd got our work cut out and plenty of it. Yet by this we'd got so sure of our little ship that we didn't worry. The chase—I call her that not because she was running away, for she wa'n't, but because we were running after her—was due ahead. I guess now, from her course, she was going to cruise off the southern coast of the States, maybe going to join Cockburn's squadron in the Chesapeake.

She was n't hurrying at all, and she likely took us for a friend, for she began just at the edge of the dark, when we were maybe two miles to windward, to signal us with lanterns. By and by, however, she quit this, for we paid no heed ; she luffed, took in sail, and aloft goes a ball that suddenly broke out into her colors. 'T was too dark to make 'em out, but they were n't the gridiron or the tricolor, that was plain.

" Union Jack, I *guess*," says a lad to me. " Well, Bill, we 'll have a closer look at the rag in a jiffy," he says, laughing.

A minute later she fired a gun towards us. 'T was a long gun I guess, and the shot hummed away in the dusk a few hundred feet across our bows. I ran below like a flash, for I had something to do before I was called to quarters. And this is what it was.

I had to get a word somehow to Nancy ; 't was no use, I could n't go on with her a doubting me, thinking me a liar. So though I 'm no fist at the writing, I made out to get a word or two on paper, and this is what it was.

"MISS NANCY BARKER—Dear lass—You wrong me cruel when you call me a liar. I never lie, and to you I never could. I kind of half cared for Lindy Truby, but the day before I shipped her father warned me I could not have her, because he found I was drunk one night, which I was and which sailors sometimes is, and no great blame thinks I. I cared so little that I was willing to ship, and next day I sent a locket and word that I was blacklisted, and said I gave up any claim I had, but maybe if I came home honorable and would lay a better course, she 'd take me again on trial, in a manner of speaking. There was no promise, lass, just a coil of 'ifs,' and then I saw you and loved you from the first, and love you now I always will. And I say this as we 're running down to fight a ship that ought to eat us up, only it 'll have to chew hard to do so, and maybe 't is the last you 'll ever hear of your loving friend,

"BILL FRY."

I went to her cabin with this letter thinking to slip it under the door. The door was open and no one inside. I stepped in to lay it on the bunk. I'd never yet been in the room of a girl I loved, and 't was a strange feeling. Her dresses that she'd made herself were hanging about, and a few other clothes. There was a kind of a perfume-like that made me think of her, and sort of turned me weak.

On a locker where the wash basin was I saw two little bracelets of cord, woven and twisted pretty, that I'd done for her. She used to wear 'em always before we had our quarrel, and now she'd taken 'em off. But it made me sorry, not mad. I'd but little time now for thinking of Nancy Barker, and I was n't going to think hard of her in what time was left. On a peg hung her jacket that she wore as a "vivandeer," and sudden the idea came to me to slip the note into its pocket. If I came out of the action, why, I'd give her word of it, if not, some day, and soon, for she often wore it, she'd put her hand in the pocket and get my letter.

So I steps over and slipped it in. And though it maybe don't sound seamanly to tell of it, much less to do it, I put my head into the flannel and kissed it a half dozen times, and felt for a minute a good deal like a boy that 's leaving home for the first time.

Then all of a sudden I heard the drums on deck bang and rattle, and I jumped and ran away forward and up through the forecastle hatch upon deck. I saw in a minute that we were in for the best fight of our lives, for not half a mile aport lay the ship we 'd picked upon, for that 's what we did, in a schoolboy's lingo, and she was a frigate.

CHAPTER X.

SHE was n't a 32—that we could tell—
she was a bigger ship than the *Essex*,
as big, I guessed at the time, and later found
was true, as the *Shannon*. I don't know why
Captain Blakely did n't sheer off when we
got near enough to see this, but I guess he 'd
made his mind up to take a frigate, and
McKnight was pushing him on if that was
needed, which the Lord knows it wa' n't.
Hardly was I on deck when across the sea
came a hail, remarkably distinct for the distance, but the wind was almost gone and the
sea very smooth.

"What ship 's that?" came the hail, and
Lieutenant Baury jumping onto the quarter
rail, yells back :

"What ship 's *that?*" and I heard a laugh

among two or three of the officers, and one
says :

" Gad, Baury, he 'll know us for Yankees
now, answering question with question,"
and in a minute the hail came again :

" Who are you, damn you ? "

" Tell 'em, Mr. Baury," says Captain Blakely, very cool, in a voice that was quiet but
heard all along the deck, and the Lieutenant shouts :

" U. S. sloop *Wasp*," and hardly was the
sound of his voice gone when she let go a
broadside.   Mostly high the balls went, but
one of 'em hit us fair in the quarter, splintered the bulwark and sent a piece of wood
flying among the officers who stood by.   It
struck one of them ; 't was poor Baury, I
think, and I saw him carried below, and
there was no more time for aught but caring
for our own guns.

Up spoke our port guns.   What they did
we could only guess, but we felt they 'd been
heard from ; and then in a minute came the
boatswain's whistle and quick orders, and

aloft went a gang of the men, the ship wore, topsails were backed, and then we seemed to be waiting.

We could see in the dusk that the enemy had come about and had tried to stand across our bows, and we knew Blakely had spoiled the move.

She could n't rake us maybe, but she had the mind to board us, and as we pushed a little ahead giving her another broadside as we went, she tacked and stood down upon us trying to run us aboard about our port beam.

But Blakely saw the game, wore ship, stood away, and beat it again. She could not come aboard us then, but she ran up, for fast she was, and no mistake; and ranging alongside, not more than pistol shot away, let us have her starboard battery, with a peppering of musketry.

'T was a well aimed broadside and brought our maintop to the deck. This was a new experience to our lads, but little time they had to sense it. As it crashed and ripped

through shrouds and ropes to the deck
hanging at last caught in the hamper of sail
and rigging, our broadside barked again, and
again we wore, for Blakely saw the enemy at
her old trick, trying to cross our bows.
Slowly we went this time, like a wounded
duck, and for a minute the thought came to
me, hot and busy as I was, that we 'd our
hands more than full this time. Again we
got her starboard guns, and again and again
we spoke back from our port battery. 'T was
not so furious and fast as in the *Reindeer*
and *Avon* fights, but 't was harder hitting,
that is, harder on us, at any rate. And when
the deep roar of the broadsides would cease
for a minute, the nasty rattle and slam of
musketry kept the dance going.

Our topmen were like all Yankee topmen,
the best of their kind, and fairly kept the
tops ablaze, but they were suffering too, and
now and again one of them would come
head first to the deck.

"Look alive," yelled my gun captain, and
hauled me to one side as I was stooping to

lift a shot, and crash on the deck, head first, came what was Dick Allen. His brains flew right and left over the men who 'd laughed with him that night at mess.

'T was but one of a dozen sights like it. We were suffering above and below, and another broadside dismounted the shifting carronade and flung it athwart its gunner, pinning him, shrieking, to the deck, like a big dog gone mad and throttling its master.

We saw it all, but could not stop to think of it. Our gun was red hot, but it had no rest, no more than we. Our crippled broadside spoke again; 't was like the voice of a man with his best teeth gone, but 't was the well known voice none the less.

"Oh, my God," says Mr. Tillinghast, who stood behind me, "if there was something to show us how she 's getting it. She must be cut up, too, she must be," he says, almost crying, brave man as he was. Ah, that was it, we knew how we were faring, but we could n't see how deep we bit.

Suddenly there came a lull, and then all

of a moment the smoke was cleft by flashes
that came from due ahead. The enemy had
run across our bows and raked us fore and
aft!

Guns leaped from their trucks, the wood
of the galley and the boats flew through the
air, men dropped about us like flies, and a
voice yelled loud and shrill—"We 've struck,
we 've struck!"

I turned and howled; what I said I don't
know, 't was blasphemy, I guess; right in
the teeth of death a man will take God's
name and never mean it, and I was not alone.
Men who were lying half dead about the gun
raised themselves and cursed.

"No, no, no!" they yelled, and a bloody
tar, whose leg was hanging by a shred
dragged himself half way across the deck.

"Where 's the cursed coward who says
we 've struck?" he cried, in a voice weak
with lost blood and husky with rage.

"Where is he, damn him? Let me get a
shot at him," then I saw him level a pistol
and fire. Some one yelled and dropped in

a heap on the deck from the shrouds where he 'd been clinging.

" 'T is Pico, the Portugee," says the gun captain to me, very quiet, the quiet of a man who saves his breath to fight with—" no *Chesapeake* business here," and just then down the deck hurries a man I 'd never known before. "Never known," say I, though 't was Captain Johnston Blakely, but a stranger was he to me in his mood this moment. His uniform was half torn away, he was black and grimy from working at some gun, his head dripped blood from a splinter wound, and nothing was bright and ship-shape aboard him but his eyes. God, how they shone!

"Get aloft, get aloft," he yelled, "leave your guns, get aloft. We must wear ship, lads, and quick, quick, quick!" he shouted, and like the great man he was, the man of hands, as well as heart and head, he jumps into the rigging, and the few of us left able to, followed him.

'T was God's mercy we were still pretty

sound above. The British had fired low for the first time in our cruise, and their good gunnery stood *us* in this time. Like a thing that goes by instinct, though sick and dying, the good *Wasp* wore, and as she wore, we came down to deck anyway, by shrouds, by ropes, by jumping and dropping, got to our gun, there was just one left of the port battery, my old pet six, and let her drive. She did n't speak again; with the discharge she burst, and my gun captain died alongside of her.

But she had her say before she went.

What she did I never knew till later, but there came a thundering sound as of powder blowing up and a cry from the frigate after it, shrill and high, and then for a minute all was still but the panting and groaning that came from the deck like the noise of a gale in the rigging.

I was not hit, nor touched even—why, I can't tell. But I was red with the blood of better men than me, and black with sweat and the grime of the best gun that ever sang in a broadside,

I looked about me. There was a little group near the quarter-deck. A knot of marines were huddled with some pikemen just abaft the mizzen, and two men stood a little apart from them. One was Blakely and one McKnight.

Just then the breeze freshened for a minute into a strange little sucking, swirling gust, the smoke lifted, and there, close alongside, lay the ship that we were fighting. Our deck was a slaughter-house, but so was theirs as well, and her sails were ribbons, her mainmast gone, and she was afire.

Cheer! How the poor lads tried to cheer when we saw it, but the noise was more like gasping. Afire she was, and her men running about like mad devils, working over the flames; but none the less we saw that she was coming aboard and that her boarders were gathered in the bows. I saw Blakely turn and hold his hand to McKnight, and then "Stand by to repel boarders," came along the deck.

'T was like the resurrection trumpet.

Men who were lying half stunned and

faint from blood staggered onto their feet, gripping the bulwarks or whatever came handy to steady by. Pikemen and marines who 'd lain close waiting for this moment jumped up. Poor beggars, they 'd seen their friends die around 'em by the score, and no hand in the game themselves. But now their turn had come, and as the frigate's bow cut upon our port quarter and her great bowsprit ripped and tore among our ropes and tackle, they ran yelling to the point where already the British were pouring aboard. They 'd stored their fight so long, our lads, they 'd boiled and raged so long inside, that they were madmen. I was with them ; every man left of the port battery was there, for the guns had gone, and our chance now lay in cutlass and pike.

'T was desperate hard fighting. Twice we beat 'em back, but the third time they came again and stronger yet. We were driven aft, inch by inch ; in a minute they 'd ha' been in possession of the ship, when the Lord sent the mizzentop, shot through and through, and heavy as lead with its weight of dead topmen, thundering into the very midst of them. Some were killed outright, some sprang into the sea to escape, some were cut off from the others and left to us, and we gave account for each man. The two ships were parallel, for the push of the frigate's bow had straightened our course, . so that we were lying in the wallow of the sea, side to side. 'T was our own chance to board, and Blakely knew it. "Boarders away," he roared, and up we swarmed.

I say swarmed, 't is but a word I use because it comes handy. There was no swarm of us, the Lord knows. But what were there were true "wasps," and had stings. Some of the lads jumped for their deck. I made a dash at an open port whose gun had been knocked off its truck. I thought there were others behind me. I heard some one climbing and panting. Some one passed me quickly, and in the smoke of the musketry that rattled from their decks, in the smoke and flying cinders of the smouldering fire,

for the British had put out the flames, a
figure like a boy's jumped by me into the
open port.

I thought 't was John Rawlins, a lad of
but eighteen; we had a number of such
aboard, and I yelled and followed after.
When, as I jumped, and landed by the dismounted gun, the figure turned, and like a
flash a cutlass swung and struck me over the
head. I fell like a log, but before the blow
took me I saw the lad was none but Nancy
Barker.

.   .   .   .   .   .

I was stunned for a few minutes, but I
came to before long, and as I raised myself
on my hands and looked out the port I saw
and heard the same noises that sang in my
ears when I went down. Musket firing and
clash of steel and shouting of seamen. We
were still alongside and I could see right out
on the deck of my old ship; 't was an easy
trick, for her bulwarks were torn away in
places like lacework. Both ships lay almost
without headway. I knew the *Wasp* had

quit minding her helm, and my thought was the enemy had as well.

"If once we could get ahead, turn and come back with our starboard guns a-bearing," I says to myself, "the game 's ours; but then if she does and we don't, it 's the end for us."

I say I thought this, if I thought anything. Sometimes I think all this came to me afterwards, for I was little better than dead as I leaned against the broken gun-truck. Everything looked like one of those toys they give children, that you turn and shake and all sorts of changes and colors come and shift and go. I saw lights flash when muskets cracked, I saw men running to and fro upon our decks. I saw them cutting and thrusting at other men—I saw them drop and I saw them sometimes stagger to their feet again. Then all would be quiet except for the noise the men would make, panting and groaning and wailing. Then all seemed to begin again, but fainter each time. As I write it now it seems to me like two men

I 've seen clinched in wrestling, resting and struggling, stopping for breath and then to it once more.

I guess I fainted again—something happened—just what, is hard to tell, but I became aware that the ships were drifting apart or we were going ahead. That was it —we were going ahead in a wind that freshened, and I knew now that the fight was over, or soon must be. The musket fire broke out afresh from above my head. I heard men calling to one another and cursing the bloody Yankees as the *Wasp* dragged by. Not a man did I see upon her decks astir. But now and again a flash would come from her foretop and a ball would whistle and spit upon the frigate's decks.

Slowly the battered sloop crept by. A lantern or two gleamed amidships, and one still swung farther aft. In the stillness, for though all was not quiet, 't was stillness alongside of what had been, I could hear the wounded and dying, and see here and there a man rolling and twisting in the death grip.

Would we escape, I wondered, would Blakely try and bring his starboard guns to use? What good was that, I thought; no men to serve 'em, and Blakely, where was he now?

Slowly the *Wasp* slipped by, and then as she drifted away into the night, I saw, standing by a stern-chaser, erect and quiet, life in every line of him, my Captain, Johnston Blakely.   Not a gun, not a pistol-shot came from sloop or frigate.   Not a word, and even the groans of the wounded seemed less to me.   Faint and hanging against the broken gun-truck, I strained my eyes after the sloop as she crept by, and the man who fought her as well as he loved her, and that is enough to say.   The wind that was getting fitful swirled a cloud of the overhanging smoke down upon the frigate.   When it lifted no *Wasp* was there.

No sound now that was n't human was to be heard, nothing but cries and groans, and now and then orders not sharp and loud, but you might almost say whispered, in voices hoarse and choked and weak.   I don't know

how the sloop pushed ahead and away, unless
't was because she was lighter and easier
drifted. I remember little more, and that
little is that I crept away myself into the
darkness of the gun-deck and among men
that groaned as I touched them in the dark,
and others that lay still and did not groan
nor speak. I seemed to recall later, a noise
as though the wind were singing high, aloft,
and that there was the roll of a heavier sea
outside.

CHAPTER XI.

HOW I CAME ON PAROLE TO PLYMOUTH TOWN.

I KNEW nothing more till I sat up in a bunk and looking around saw faces I did n't recognize and knew that I had n't been dreaming.

" Be quiet now, my man," said a voice behind me, "you 're going to pull through—thick head-pieces you Yankees carry about —now then, lie still ; yes, you 're a prisoner, if you want to know, aboard His Majesty's frigate, *Sardis*, and we 're being pretty careful of you, for you 're the only one we 've got. Now then, lie quiet, for there 's some questions got to be asked you by and by."

The man who spoke to me was a surgeon —rough he was, but a kind man, too. I lay quiet, what else was there to do, and what with a buzz in my head that whirled and had bright colors in it when I stirred much, my mind did but little work all that day, and this was three days after our fight, they told me later. But next day I was more myself, and the surgeon, Carr was his name, told me the Captain was coming to talk to me.

Now here 's a strange thing to tell,—whether I was cracked in mind as well as head; whether my weakness and the flurry of a British bigwig a pumping me, got hold of me, I don't know, but sink me if I could remember what ship I 'd been on or where I 'd been cruising, or how long. All that would come to me was that I 'd served aboard the *Essex*, and 't was her I thought the *Sardis* had engaged.

"My man," says the British captain, "what 's your ship?"

"The *Essex*, your honor," says I.

"Don't lie, you hound," he says, very hot. "The *Essex* was took five months ago. Where have you been cruising?"

"The South Seas, your honor."

He ripped out an oath. "I'll find a way to make you tell the truth," says he, "if you try that game again with me," he says. "Now your ship was the *Wasp*, your captain was Blakely, you've been in the Channel Chops and off Fayal, so you see I know all that. Now tell me what weight of metal did ye carry?"

"We had thirty-two guns, sir."

"Ah," he says, chuckling, "Carr, 't was as good as a frigate, and but little lighter than us. Go on?"

"We'd 255 men aboard, for a few were in the *Essex Junior*."

"You damn Yankee," he shouted, jumping up. "Did you hear me? You'll get ten dozen if you don't stow your bloody lies about the *Essex*. Now harkye, no more. What's your weight, tell me and tell me true."

I lay back on the bed. It's God's own truth, I couldn't get to my mind what he wanted me to. The *Essex* was clear enough, but the *Wasp* wasn't even as much as a

dream. I guess I looked pretty pale and
badly used up, for Mr. Carr speaks out :

"Captain," he says, "this man's too weak
to talk to like a well man—he's maybe a
stubborn dog, but leave him to me, I'll get
word from him," he says, and the Captain
left us. Later in the day, the Surgeon comes
in and sits down by me and gives me a drink
of something that hearts me up a bit.

"Now," says he, "my man, I'll tell you
what went on four nights ago, and maybe, as
a lawyer'd say, ''t will refresh your memory.'

"At seven o'clock we sighted a ship, corvette build, that came down fast and steady
to us. Later we signalled with lanterns and
got no answer. Then by and by we
hailed and got reply that 't was the United
States sloop-o'-war, *Wasp*. Now," says he,
"don't that jog your memory?"

"Well," says he, for I lay still, not yet getting my bearings, "about nine o'clock we
engaged you and there was hell's delight for
the next hour and a half. We shot your
main top off and the mizzen as well, and

raked you fore and aft, and you set us afire
and carried away our mainmast, silenced our
starboard battery and played the devil among
the Leslies generally," says he, " now do you
get into the wind ?   Not yet, hay ? "

" Then we boarded and came back again,
and then you came aboard through a port,
don't you remember now, and got your nut
sliced as you came. What, you beggar,
don't you take yet ? "

" Doctor," says I, " I know there 's something I can't bring back—I know it 's there,
and I guess what you say is likely it, but I
can't, so help me, patch it up."

" Well, well," says he, " as long as you
give up your yarn about the *Essex* you 're
getting along.   But I say, my man," says he
suddenly, as if an idea had struck him,
" don't you remember a pretty lass as had
been aboard your ship—Nancy Barker ? "

Ah, it was coming back now, coming so
that I put my hands across my face and
groaned and twisted on the bunk. 'T was
coming back, that fearful night, the bloody

ruck of the *Wasp's* deck, the useless guns burst or dismounted, the swivel carronade atop its gunner, the burning frigate, and the falling topmast, my leap into the port, and my last sight of Nancy as she swung her cutlass round.

When a little time had gone and I took my hand from my face and looked at the Surgeon, he knew from my eyes that the compass was lighted again and I could lay a course. He sat back in his chair and laughed a bit ; he was a kind man, though rough.

" By the Lord," says he, " there 's human nature ! A woman's name will bring back what even a tale of glory won't—for lad," says he, leaning over towards me, " I 'm a loyal servant of King George, but I can admire pluck and courage in an enemy, all the more if he 's got much the same blood as I, and I tell you 't was glory, glory, no less, that your Captain, God rest him, wherever he is, got three days agone. You 're smaller than we, I know well," says he, " and yet 't was nip and tuck. Now then, can you tell us what your metal was, the girl was too shaken up to just recall."

' The girl," I cries, " Nancy ! "

" Aye, aye," says he, looking sharp at me, "the lass we put aboard the *Cawnpore,* Indiaman, the day after the fight, her and our wounded—we kept you, my boy, for information, and we wanted it bad enough to give you a cabin to yourself so as to save your precious hide, for that same," says he, laughing again, " so just loosen up and let 's have a little now."

" Just one thing, Doctor," says I very quiet, " did she know I was aboard ? "

" She ? 'T aint likely ! You were never found till she 'd left the ship. You were stowed away under a devil's own hamper of truck, and came within an ace of going over-board in a canvas nightshirt too—but come, come, Captain Henderson's waiting for that information, speak up, my lad, and lively as may be.   What was your armament ? "

" Eleven guns broadside, stern-chasers, and a swivel carronade, sir."

"Come, come, don't lie to me," says he, very stern.

"As God 's my judge," I says, raising my right hand.

He gave a long whistle—"Well, and how many men?"

"One hundred and sixty-eight, sir."

He got up and took a step about the cabin, there was room for but just one step, and then sat down.

"What 's your name?" says he.

"Bill Fry, sir."

"Where born?"

"Biddeford."

"Oh ho, a Devon man—I daresay there were plenty more English aboard the *Wasp* as well?"

I got a little hot, weak as I was.

"Doctor," says I, "I 'm from Biddeford, true enough, but the Biddeford I hail from is in the State of Maine, and as for the rest of the crew, barring a yellow cur of a Portugee, that Bob Lowther shot dead for cowardice in the action with you, the crew was

American from New England to the last
man," I says. "Captain Blakely was from
Ireland, came over a baby," says I.

"Well, well, well, be cool!" says he, quite
friendly, "it 's all the same blood whichever
way. And I 'm glad Blakely was Irish," says
he, "for I 'm that myself, and I swear," says
he, "my lad, it 's proud I am he did n't
strike your blasted old gridiron, too," says
he.

"What, sir?" says I, "did n't you take the
Wasp?"

"Take her! Not a bit," says he, "don't
you remember,—but of course, poor devil,
how could you?—she slipped away and the
wind came up heavy; she was drifting only,
I fancy, but though we looked for her in the
morning—for Captain Henderson 's a game
man, though I don't like him," says he, half
to himself, "and was bound he 'd have her at
last. She was out of sight at daybreak, and,
Bill," says he, quite solemn, for my face
showed how I felt, "a ship crippled like
her makes sail and goes fast to just one port,

Davy Jones's, God rest 'em," he adds, " what
was left of 'em ! "

I could n't say a word, but turned on my
side. I saw again my last sight of my dear
old ship,—for I 'd got to love her next to
Nancy ; aye, that 's a true word,—and the
face of Captain Blakely looking at us from
the quarter-deck, quiet, but unafraid and un-
beaten, as the sloop crawled away.

" Bill," says the Surgeon, as he got up to
go, " I 'll try to have you put aboard some
ship bound to England if we meet one—
you 've money, I see." I had slipped some
and my little log-book inside my shirt when
we went into action—sometimes I think
't was a forethought of what was to come
made me do so.

" Well, money and a civil tongue will keep
you safe enough in Old England till this
family row is done. Let me give you just
a word of advice. If Captain Henderson
asks you how big you were, say you carried
sixteen guns broadside and three hundred
men. The lie will make your life aboard

here easier, and trust Manners's crew, when the news gets out, to prove 't is a lie," and so he left me.

Well, a couple of days later I was put aboard a brig, the *Calypso*, from Cadiz to Plymouth, and the *Sardis* went on into the harbor of Cadiz which we were very near. I never saw nor heard of Dr. Carr again. He was a kind, humane man, and I guess a brave one. He and all aboard the *Sardis* went down in a great gale off Tarifa, trying to stand around to Gibraltar to refit there.

'T is not a Christian way, but barring that Dr. Carr went down along with his ship, the thought that the little *Wasp* and my old gun number six, made the *Sardis* the easy food she was for the storm, comes to me again and again and makes me proud.

Well, we had bad winds or none, and on the 26th of October, 1814, they put me ashore in Plymouth .town, thin and white and shaky, twenty-five sovereigns in my pockets and a hate for everything I saw in my heart, for all this time I 'd been baited

and jeered at and called "Yankee," till I
almost hated the good old word. And I
thought and thought of Nancy Barker and
fought down each day the fearful question
that came into my mind. And this is what
that question was, for 't was with me many
a long night and day :

"Did Nancy know 't was me she cut
down? If she did, why," thinks I, "I love
her ever so dear, even if so be our courses
cross again, that ends it all, but if 't was only
at one of the *Wasp's* crew hap-hazard, and
not at Bill Fry she struck, why when I find
her, for find her will I, to take or leave I 'm
hers."

And I went from one tack to the other
day in and out, now thinking the worst of
her and now almost crying to myself as I
thought of her pluck in jumping aboard the
Sardis, and swinging her cutlass so handsome.

Well, I was some days in Plymouth lying
quiet, in a tavern where seafaring men were
used to stay. There were plenty of them there,

the house was noisy, and I can't say for my life why I went to the place, for 't was certain to be known soon that I was American, but seamen will get together whether friends or not, and so to the "Anchor" came I.

They gave me a pretty good sort of a room for I showed a fist full of the yellow boys, and for a few days I kept my bunk. Then I began to itch to get below and see the lads that every night I heard roaring songs, and now and again cursing the Yankees and the French. Why they were cursing the French just then I could n't tell, for the two nations were at peace, but I guess 't was a habit picked up in the long war, and a sort of second nature.

My head troubled me some days, but I did n't give it much thought. I had my strength yet, or part of it, for one day a swab comes lurching against my door, and says he:

"You bloody Yankee pirate, come on deck," says he, "and I 'll break your head over again for you," he says.

I just flung the door back and got him by

the neck and under the right arm and slung him down stairs. He fell hard but he was n't hurt, and by and by when he 'd got through cursing, he goes away.

I suppose he told a lot of mates below, for soon up comes three or four and raps at my door.

" Come," says I, and picks up an old pistol I 'd bought the day I came ashore. Well, they meant no harm, and were quite civil spoken.

" Mate," says one, " we hear as how you are an American seaman, and knowing this war is still a-going, we 'd like to know just how you come to be loose in Plymouth," says he.

" Well, mate," says I, " seeing you 're civil and don't want to break my head, I 'll tell you. I have here," and I pulls it out, " a parole from Captain Henderson of the *Sardis*, if you know his fist."

One steps up. " I know it well," says he, " for I was purser's clerk aboard a ship he served on once, and that 's it all right."

"Well," says the first one, "there's no news come of the *Sardis* taking any Yankee warship, perhaps ye'll tell us how you come to be captured?"

"Come below," says the man who'd been purser's clerk and who was a bit decenter dressed and cleaner looking than the others. "Come below and we'll have a go of rum or so. You'll be treated respectful and fair, lad," says he to me, "my word on that."

So down we went. There was quite a crowd in the tap-room, and I saw as soon as I'd got set down to a table that I was a curiosity. We got our rum, and one—the man who'd first asked me of my being in Plymouth and whose name was Hood—says, says he:

"Here's to King George's navy, and to hell with——" I don't know what he was going to say, but the ex-purser's clerk calls out:

"Hold your tongue, Hood," says he, "fair play's a jewel, and here's a wounded man, a Yankee, a drinking with us, and say what any man will, the American navy's little, but it's the right seed for a big plant, by thunder, and here's to all good mariners who talk King George's English, if you want the old boy in the toast," says he, and we drank around.

Well, pretty soon the man who took our part, and who was called Mr. Stevens by the others, says: " Now, mate," says he, " tell us how you come to be with us. Jack always likes a yarn, and I 'll go bail you have a good one to spin," says he.

" Well," says I, for we 'd had a couple of rounds by then and I was warming up, " I 'll tell you how it was, Mr. Stevens and mates and all," says I very friendly, for if there 's bad temper in much rum, there 's lots of good humor in a fair load as well, " 't was this a way.   I was able-bodied seaman aboard the *Wasp*——"

" The *Wasp*," shouts Hood, " the *Wasp*, eh. John," he yells to the tavern-keeper, " here 's a man from the *Wasp* as took the *Bon Accord* and lost you a neat venture, John."

At this the man came cursing across the floor and pushed up against me.

"What," says he, "is this one of the Yankee pirates? What 's he doing here, I wonder?" says he, cursing and shaking his hand at me. A lot of the others joined in, and there was noise and oaths enough for a spell. Mr. Stevens had been kind of took back, I guess, when he heard I was off the *Wasp*, and you 'd think, to hear the swabs, that the little sloop had bankrupted half Plymouth; but now he jumps up and says, "Stow this, stow this," says he, "here 's a coil about a wounded man on parole; don't ye see, you fools," he says, "that if this man 's a prisoner on parole the ship he served on 's taken or sunk?"

Well, this quieted them a bit, but it stirred me up.

"Easy, sir," says I, "easy, all. I boarded the *Sardis* in the fight," says I, "was cut down, and when the two crafts drew away from each other I was lying helpless aboard the British ship. Taken, the *Wasp* was *not*,

16

nor could n't be," says I, " by any king's
ship that floats," and here I got up and
elbowed the tavern-keeper, who 'd been
cursing me, so he nearly fell across a table,
" sunk she may be, but the gridiron 's at her
peak, and you swabs may tie right up to
that," says I, and picked up a chair, for the
crowd was all going to come aboard.

But Stevens, who had a handy way of
speech with him and some kind of a hold
like, in the tavern, got 'em quiet, and says to
me, "You 're a Yankee, sure enough, my
man," says he, " for you 've got the gift of
the brag," says he.

"Which they brought with 'em from England, and left plenty and to spare to home,
at that," says I.

He laughed. " You 're a blooming impu-
dent beggar," says he, " but I like you,
and *I* don't say what *you* say of brag aint
true. But tell us more of the *Wasp*; we
know about the bloody little craft, but we
want to hear more."

Now, just as he spoke, into the tavern

comes another man, dressed like a gentleman, in top-boots and carrying a whip.
"Stevens," says he, "I 'm glad to find you ;
I rode in from Bideford to-day, and there 's
a show there 't would please all good mariners.   And who 's running it, d' ye think?
Why, old Barker's girl, Nancy, who used to
help tend at this old 'Anchor,' " says he.

"Who?" says I, almost tipping the table
as I jumped up.   Then I sat down sudden
for I thought my best way to get news was
to keep a close mouth and listen.

"Why, Nancy Barker, my man," says he,
"don't you know her?   Every man who 's
paid for a pint in this inn knows *her*—but,
Stevens," says he, paying no more attention
to me, "it 's the show that pleases me.
She 's got a house wagon that she travels in,
and letters on the outside calling her 'Gunner Nancy,' and saying she 'll give the true
account of how the famous Yankee ship,
Wasp, was sunk, and how she took part in
the action, and—listen to this—that she will
exhibit a fearful cutlass encounter between

herself and one of the crew of the *Wasp*, a
Yankee on parole, who is part of the show.
How 's that for brass? She 'd ever her share,
the vixen, but this tops all."

Well, I could have struck him for his tone,
and I could have cried for the thoughts that
sprang into my mind. But I held myself
down and Stevens and the others gave a
shout. When they 'd eased on laughing
Stevens says:

" Why, Squire," he says, " this lad here 's
a Wasp himself, and claims to have seen the
last of his ship and got a sliced coxcomb
into the bargain," says he.

" What," says the Squire, " is it so? Well,
my man, you 'll remember Nancy, then, for
she says she was aboard the *Wasp* a prisoner
three months—a nice sort of prisoner I 'll
go bail, and one your Captain would n't be
in a hurry to exchange," says he with a
grin.

" Sir," says I, getting onto my feet, "there
was a lass of that name aboard the *Wasp*,
and she was as safe there, so far as decent

treatment goes, as she would be here in her native town, aye," and now my temper came into the wind, " and from what I see I guess a damn sight safer."

" Oh," says he, quite cool and sneering, " you are n't talking to the marines, my man, I *guess* not," says he, mocking me. " A likely tale that," says he; " don't preach your Yankee cant to us—what do you know of the ways of the ward-room—your Captain had a good eye for a good figure," says he, and the next minute my glass broke across his face.

Well, I can't remember all that took place then. I recall a mix up of cursing and pot throwing, of my swinging a stool about my head, of getting hit from front and behind, of Stevens howling " fair play " from atop the table, of the Squire grappling with me and flinging me out of the room under the stars, and then all was black for a while.

When I came to, a man was washing my face for me and gave me a drop from a flask. " What 's wrong?" says I, quite weak; then when the man spoke I knew 't was the purser's clerk.

"You poor devil," says he, "they 've man-handled you and no mistake," says he, "but you 're the biggest fool alive, I 'm thinking. Now, if you 've ever a bundle upstairs, I 'll fetch it for you here, don't ye stir till I come, don't go back into the tap-room, or they 'll maybe kill you. I 'll get your kit and you 'd best tramp. Get out of this town and keep out, for the place is no fit one for a man that can't hold his tongue with his life on the game. Don't stir till I come back."

Off he goes and I began to feel myself over. I 'd been kicked and beat and mauled, but no great harm was done, though my old wound had bled a bit. I was stiff and sore, but well minded to get out of Plymouth if I had to foot it. I felt for my purse, and 't was still in my breeches pocket. In a minute Stevens came back with my bundle.

"Now," says he, " Bill Fry, you 'd best be moving. Keep straight down the alley and

you 'll hit the street; bear to the nor'west
and you 'll be in the country in half an hour.
There 's not such a bad inn at Meavey, 'The
Plowshare,' and you can put up there for
the night; but get out of this neighborhood
as soon as may be," says he.

"Thankee, kindly," says I; "you 're a
man, sir, and a seaman," says I; "and I
hope I may some time do a good turn by
you; one thing, sir," says I, "is it the Bideford road?"

He looked at me, and I thought in the
dim light he was laughing. "Looking for
the lass, eh?" says he; "leave her alone,
my lad, for a shrew she always was and
always will be."

"One thing, sir," says I; "shrew she may
be, but I 've heard tell she was honest."

"Oh, you have, eh?" said he, and then he
laughed, but kindly like, "well," says he,
"as you Yankees say, I *guess* she is, I only
guess you understand. She was always a
good enough lass, bar her temper, but vixen
and shrew she is, my boy, and—good luck to

you," says he, as he shook my hand and
turned away towards the inn.

By ten that night, nigh dropping with
weariness, I came to the " Plowshare " at
Meavey, and for sight of a couple of crowns
got lodging and a supper. Next morning,
stiff as I was, I was out and headed along
the pike for Bideford. 'T was a sweet day,
cool and bright. The fields were like our
fields in spring, and now and again I 'd see
roses blooming plenty. Folks eyed me close
sometimes, and some would cross the road
as I came by. I guess I looked hard, and if
I looked what I felt I must ha' been no
pleasant man to see.

If 't was fine weather outside there was
foul in my heart. Here was a rough-tongued
young swab talking of Nancy as if she were
all that I would give my life to ha' kept her
from. Here was she a-travelling about with
some man in tow, bold as brass, likely to be
insulted any time and, as I write now, I can
remember what I felt when it came to me
then, that maybe she could n't rightly be

insulted, and was no better than she 'd be taken for. I wished a dozen times I 'd shot her as she swung her cutlass over me in the *Sardis* frigate, aye, and laid myself dead along-side. But see her I 'd made up my mind to. I 'd ask her two or three things, come what would. And I almost forgot my wound and my bruises as I limped along in the dust.

That night I slept at a tavern just outside the town of Okehampton. The next day's jog would fetch me into Bideford.

CHAPTER XII.

HOW I FOUND NANCY, AND DROPPED ANCHOR.

THE next day was another fair one. 'T was market day, too, and there were many carts upon the road. Once in a while I'd get a ride; one farmer knowing me for a sailor, took me from Merton to Torrington, nigh on to six miles, I should guess, so I made good time.

At Torrington, outside the " White Boar " tavern, I stood talking a little with the old lad who 'd given me a lift, but who would take nothing for it but a double pint of ale, when up rolls a coach with a lot of jolly, handsome-dressed bucks a-top. They shouted for liquor, and a neat-looking girl came out to serve 'em. After they 'd drunk and joked with the lass, and lighted up pipes, and were

about to drive on, one of them whose sleeve
hung loose caught sight of me.

"Hold on, Dick," says he to the buck
driving, "let me have a word or two with
that fellow yonder."

("Bill," says I to me, "keep your temper
and talk smooth and respectful.")

"Here, you," calls he, "you 're a seaman,
what are you doing inshore when there 's a
bloody war on the seas?" says he.

"Beg your pardon, sir," says I, "but I 'm
only going down Bideford way, on a short
leave, to see a friend," said I, "and I 've a
bit of cut here, sir, that keeps me ashore
awhile." I lifted my hat and let them see
the bloody bandage across my crown.

"Well, well," said the gentleman with one
arm, in a softer voice, "I see you 're no shirk,
which I swear I took you for. Where did
the cutlass come from that gave you that?"

"From a Yankee ship, sir; do you know
the *Wasp?*"

"Do I know her, begad?" says he, with a
laugh; "look at this," and he swung his

sleeve in the air; "I lost that aboard the *Reindeer*."

The look on my face as he said this would have made him wonder, I guess, but just then, "Oh, come, come, George," calls two or three on the coach, "we 'll be late for the fun, and we 've heard about that *Reindeer* fight too often already; stow it, as you sailors say—Drive on, Dicky." And the coach rolled away, the gentleman with the one arm swearing plenty at his friends and they a-laughing and swearing a stave or two themselves.

"They be gay lads," says the farmer that had given me the lift, "and one of them, the boy with the arm gone, was officer aboard one of the King's ships and lost his arm in a sea-fight. He lives with his father, old Sir George, back of Yarborough—Warmouth Hall is the place—They 'll be going, those lads to hear the lass talk and play broad-swords,—the one who calls herself Gunner Nancy, you 'll maybe have seen her down Plymouth way?"

"No," says I, "she 's not been there yet,

but tell me, mate, what kind of a raree show 't is," says I, hoping to get a little news from the old lad.

" Why," says he, " the lass goes about in her little house wagon and there 's a chap travels with her, he drives a bit cart behind," (Ah, thinks I, that 's better) " and carries her tent and fixings. Then she ups with the tent and puts a kind of stage like before it, and lectures, as you might say, about the war with the Yankees, and how she was a prisoner aboard the *Wasp*, and how she got away and whipped a chap as chased her ; then out comes the lad that 's with her and they fight a round or two with wooden cutlasses, and then down he drops and that is the end. 'T is a proper fine show," said the old lad, " and a pretty lass too," says he, a wagging his head, " but I doubt she 's a vixen," says he.

I left the old man at Torrington and footed it the rest of the way to Bideford. At the south end of the town I saw a tavern and I went in and got a long glass of ale.

"Where's this show of the sailor lass?" says I to the barmaid.

She looked me over and laughed. "You mean Gunner Nancy," says she, "why just beyond the bridge in an open bit, a common like," says she—"half the King's navy's been along this way to see her," says she, laughing again, "and I can't tell why, the bold, forward creature she is."

I did n't listen to more, but was out and down the road again, and not long after came to the bridge and crossed. I saw a crowd in an open lot, I saw a little round tent, and behind it a wagon rigged like a house on wheels and big signs swinging down its sides.

"Gunner Nancy," the biggest of the signs read.

"She will tell of her long captivity aboard the Yankee sloop-of-war the *Wasp*. How that ship at last was sunk by H. B. M. F. *Sardis*, and how she made her escape, cutting down and taking prisoner a Yankee who pursued her. He is now on parole and attached to the entertainment, and will engage in a fearful cutlass encounter with his fair captor."

Here was enough to make a dead man laugh, but there was no laugh in me. I 'd given up trying to reason out what Nancy, with her show and her follower and her stories about the *Wasp*, and taking a Yankee prisoner might have got to be ; gone wrong or gone mad, I could not think which. But I 'd made up my mind to see her and speak with her, if but for a moment, and that I was set on. As I slipped in among the crowd about the platform in front her tent I saw many of them were seafaring men, and in the first row I saw the bucks who 'd driven past me at Torrington. They were a jolly crew and quite tipsy some of 'em, by now.

The crowd was a noisy one and kept shouting, " Nancy ! Nancy ! Gunner ! Gunner ! " till presently the flaps of the tent opened and she came out and curtseyed.

Aye, 't was Nancy Barker, none other. She looked older, and sadder, yes and thin-

ner, but 't was she. I turned half faint as I
looked at her and lurched heavy against an
old boy to my right, who damned me, and
told me to stop fouling of him.

There was something about the lass that
cut me to the heart and yet made me almost
wild with happiness. 'T was in her face.
She 'd bow and smile and strut up and down
the little stage, and maybe those who 'd
never seen her really smile thought her face
was always as it was this day, and that look
on it meant nothing and was always there.
I knew better. I 'd seen her face when she
was happy and 't was never the one she
carried with her as she waited for the crowd
to get still and begin her yarn. And at
times a glance would come into her eye that
I saw there the day Josh Sewall died and I
knew she 'd not forgotten yet ; and little as
it was,—to know that she still remembered
me, for I felt sure 't was so, seemed for the
time enough for me, be she what she might.

As soon as the crowd got half-way quiet
she began. I can't give here all that she

said, but 't was a lingo learned like a Poll-
parrot's.   I'd ha' laughed hearty at some of
it had it not been Nancy, and had there
been a laugh left in the locker, which there
was n't, for 't was ruck and rubbish.

"She's never writ that herself," thinks I,
"too many words, and too little truth for a
lass like her."   Why, she'd speak of the
Yankees as if we could n't fight, and then in
the same breath she'd tell how we'd cut the
Reindeer into matchwood and sunk the *Avon*.
How we could be such bloody cowards as
her speech made out we were, and yet do as
good work, beat me, but Lord, it pleased all
the crowd, the sailors chief, and they cheered
and shouted to her and chucked sixpences
and shillings on to the platform.

Then Nancy would bow and smile, that
smile that came and went without ever
knowing what her heart was thinking of.

I saw my gentleman with the one arm
did n't care much for this.   Once when one
of his friends hit him a clap on the shoulder
and asked him why he did n't cheer, he said

17

something very short. Well, so the thing
ran on. She told about the *Wasp's* crew, its
officers, and its guns. I found we carried
22 guns a broadside and 350 men in our
crew, and "of course," as a couple of chaps
near me said, "of course we could whip a
brig like the *Reindeer* easy."

By and by she came to the last fight.
'T was not so near the truth as the rest. The
hand that wrote the *Reindeer* and *Avon* en-
gagements might ha' seen 'em, but never
that last grapple in the night. One thing
she did tell true, and that was the minute's
space that she sprang aboard the *Sardis* and
I after.

" 'T was this way," ran her yarn, so near
as I can repeat, "the Yankee sloop was helpless. She would not mind her helm, her
port guns were all dismounted, and she had
one hope, and that was to come aboard. A
wild hope and a mad one, gentlemen all, for
a Yankee to ever think to carry a King's
ship by boarding. At long bowls they may
be good, but foot to foot, hand to hand,

steel to steel, no man can stand against a true Briton."

Of course there was a shout and a cheer at this. I heard the one-armed boy say to another, "That's a blooming bounce, but she's a pretty shrew!"

"Just as they called 'Boarders away!' I sprang up the hatchway," goes on Nancy, "I ran to the port bulwarks, such as were left of them, and sprang into one of the ports of the *Sardis*. A sailor from the *Wasp* leaped at the same moment, and I turned and in a flash drew my cutlass and——" As she said this the flaps of the tent flew open, and a man rigged in American seaman's togs runs out and they began a sort of broadsword play.

There was great laughing and cheering. You'd ha' supposed 't was all dead earnest, and aboard the *Sardis*, to hear them cheer the girl and curse the poor devil who took the part of the Yankee. As for me I was two parts angry to hear us miscalled as we had been, and yet with it all was a feeling,

"I 'll do that, sir, thanks to you," says I, and I looked at Nancy again. She was so white and scared looking, and her hands that had hid her eyes were clutching now at her throat. I pitied her till I looked again at the sneak at her feet, who did not dare look me in the eye.

"One thing I 'll ask," says I, "gentlemen, with your permission—I 'll ask this lady if I 'm not Bill Fry, of the sloop *Wasp*."

There was a stir at this, you may lay to that, but 't was nothing to the yell that went up when the girl said in a kind of whisper, "Yes, 't is true, you are."

Well, there was another dash for me—men cursed and struck at me. The young officer and his friends formed around me, but in spite of this I was hit again and again with sticks and canes.

"Let us have 'im, Mr. George, give him up," yelled the crowd, "we 've all a score to pay the Yankee pirate, give him to us."

"Give him to you, you cowards!" yells the lad back; "scores to pay, do you say?

Why, have n't I a score against the *Wasp* as well? Look at this sleeve! I have a score to pay some day at sea like a man, not by kicking and mauling and pounding an unarmed man, fifty to one," says he. " Get back, get back,—you know me, and you know my father; get back, or some one will be laid by the heels!" says he. " Now, my man," he says to me, " jump on the platform and say your say."

I crawled on to the staging and staggered to my feet—I am obstinate and want to go through with what I begin, and winded as I was I says, catching my breath now and again :

" I am one of the *Wasp's* crew, and I 'm proud of it."

" Hold your Yankee brag, curse you ! " yells a man.

" You 've a right to be proud," says the young officer. " Stop your blasted noise, Robbins," says he to the man who cursed me.

" And I saw the *Reindeer* fight, I was in

it, and all the lass says is true.   Only this, if
the Yankees are cowards, what praise is it
for Manners's men to make such a fine fight
when the odds were but three to two,"
says I.

"A good point, a good point," says the
officer, "I can swear they 're no cowards.
I was there myself."

"And I saw our sloop sink the *Avon*, and
I was in the *Sardis* fight," I goes on, "and
right here I want to say, mates and gentlemen, that the lass is not fair to herself, not
fair at all. 'T was *true* she sprang into the
port of the frigate, as she says. 'T was *true*
a Yankee sailor followed her. 'T was *true*
she turned and cut him down, but 't is *not*
true that that man there, lying at her feet,
a sneak who deserted his ship before the
fight, was the man who followed. His line
is n't boarding ships, mates, not his. Little
credit to her to cut down that poor spirited
swab—no ; the man she struck was a man,
a man, mates and gentlemen, and an able-
bodied seaman, and his name is mine. It 's

Bill Fry, and here 's the mark of her cutlass yet," and I staggered and half sank to my knees. I did n't know what was up till, as I took my hat off and pushed up the bandage to show the cut, a stream of blood poured down my face. A blow from some stick had done it.

I did n't exactly faint, for I remember what took place then. I see yet the look of horror and self-reproach on Nancy's face as she listened, and the tears that went down her cheeks, her lips that quivered, and the smile they tried to form, as she ran to me when I tottered, and kneeled and flung her arms around me.

" Mates," she cried, in her old way, " I hear it now. 'T is my true love, Bill Fry—a Yankee, maybe, but a brave, true, kind mariner that I 've been dying for ever since I thought him gone. 'T is I struck him, mates, but I did 't know him in the smoke and the smother, and the wound that 's been in my heart, lads, since I thought him dead is deeper yet."

This I remember, almost word for word,
and little else except the crowd a-cheering,
and the young officer shaking my hand and
Nancy's and cheering and crying as well.

.   .   .   .   .   .

'T is fifteen years since this took place.
Fifteen years since Nancy and I found each
other again. She 'd started her little show
and lecture to make her living. She landed
desperate, wretched, her money—the little
she had—on the *Wasp*, and nothing in her
pocket but my letter. 'T was this she read
over and over and believed one hour and
doubted the next, but she wore it close to
her heart, she told me.

One day Jim Downs, who was hanging
about Bideford, saw her sign and looked for
her. She knew him then for what he was,
yet as a venture they agreed to fix up the
little show together (he wrote the yarn she
spoke, as I suspicioned), but they were
partners only that far.

"Will," says she, "I don't want you to

ask me if that coward has ever been more to me than a kind of hired servant, and a dummy man," says she. " I 'd despise you if you could ask me such a question, but as you want to know so bad," says she, kissing me, " I 'll say that he was no more to me than a dog, nor so much, for I 'll kiss my dog, Boxer, and that 's more than ever I did for Jim Downs, nor so much as touched him, except with my foot, in the cutlass fight," she says.

Yes, 't is many a long year since then. What came to Downs I never knew. He sneaked out of Bideford, and he never showed face to me again. Nancy and I were married in two weeks. " Short courtship," says Sir George as now is, the young officer who stood my friend and who swore he 'd give the bride away, if only for a chance to kiss her.

" Short, sir," says I, " not so very. We were courting a bit on the *Wasp*, when we were n't fighting," I says.

" It 's best short then," say he, " on the

present tack, for the Lord knows when you 'll
begin fighting again." But 't was his joke,
that is all.

One might think, maybe, that two people,
as quick to pay away on the temper as
Nancy and I, would ha' found catspaws and
chopped seas in our course plenty. But
't was not so. The day we were married she
says to me, says Nancy:

" Will—I 'll *try*, that 's the best I can say,
to be a good mate for you," she says.

" Mate! lass," says I, " you 'll be captain—
not mate," says I, joking, "that 's *my* rank,"
I says.

" No, dear, you 're to command," says she,
and then for a spell we argufied, till at last
we agreed to both command, and both obey
orders, and our ship with its two captains
never struck foul weather or shoal water.

I was minded at first to go home, but Nancy
had such a love for England, and I can't
blame her, and I was n't needed at home ;
and when Sir George Warmouth offered me
the post of lodge-keeper to him I went.

'T is not a bad job—slow at times and dull, but easy for one as has a bad nick in his crown. Hard work, or work at sea, I never could do again. Oh, the times I 've dreamed of the fresh salt smell, of the snore of the gale in the shrouds, of the pleasant heel and dip of a clipper ship. But no more of that for Bill Fry. When I 'm old, if I have a bit laid by, I 'll go to where I can see the blue water each day and each hour. Now I 'll do what I may to keep a place that 's a good one, all round.

My little lass has grown to be a big girl now with a spice of her mother's spirit—her mother that 's gone these five years—but not her face—there was never—will never be again in God's round world, a face like Nancy Barker's to Bill Fry.

My boy is going in a few years, to follow the sea—as far as old New England, there to be what he can't be here—as good as the next man, and a Yankee.

THE END.